The Last Sheep

Chris Ringler

[4]

Table of Contents

The Weeping Widow

7

Part One

41

The Black Machines

178

Part Two

186

The Warlocks

298

Part Three

304

Part Four

359

Happily Ever After

377

The Weeping Widow

Every land is a map made of stories, a tapestry of tales that carry the weight of history and weaves it into the future moment by moment by moment. Every great love, small pain, catastrophic war, or miniscule triumph all becomes part of the larger story of the world though these are tales that we may never know. There is an ocean of stories and a sky full of tales but not every story sees the light of history. There is such a story that has been lost for a great many years, forgotten through the ages and perhaps purposely so because some stories wear a shroud so dark that it seems better to let them go than to dwell on them. I tell you though that every story is a part of us, every tale a piece of our hearts, and to let these things go is to ignore the very things that make all of us, who we are.

No tale should be forgotten.

None.

Because every tale, even the smallest, echoes throughout the ages.

And every story carries with it the tremors that may yet shake the world.

And this friend is a story of an earthquake yet to come.

There was a time in the Land when the sky was black with war and the ground red with blood. This was a time when humans were still struggling to live on two legs and to behave with their minds and not their instincts. It was a time when passions drove kingdoms to war again and again. And it was the beginning of a change that many still fight against to this day. Some said it was a kiss that had begun this grand war, a kiss between two lovers who were forbidden their love yet pursued their heart's desires against the wishes of their families and the wisdom of their elders, a great love and a simple kiss. But it was a forbidden love and a forbidden kiss and it had been seen by a spiteful person more interested in personal ambition than such a thing as Love and with their jealousy at this love and their poisoned words in the ear of the parents of these loves and thus began the war. First it was small, between families, and crops were burned, and farm animals were killed, and eventually fights broke out but none of it raised much attention from the surrounding communities until the father of one family was killed accidentally during a brutal fight. Things seemed to calm down after this and the families seemed to realize the folly of their ways but it was too late. The King of one of the lands was childhood friend of the dead father and the King declared that the family that had done this crime must all be put to death. When the King of their land heard of this demand he had his soldiers gather and guard the boundaries of the land. Outraged the other King declared war on the neighboring land and so war was had and when a war is started it is very hard to stop. The blood boils, the eyes narrow, and the lust for violence cannot be quelled but sometimes there are outside influences that fan the flames into an inferno. The lovers were killed, their families were killed, and even the person who had started it all with their whispers found themselves on the wrong side of a blade. It was a black time and no matter how hard the royal advisors tried to calm their kings they could not get them to listen, and by the time the kings did realize what they had begun it was too late to stop it. The war had become a living thing and it would not be easily stopped.

War is an animal, a hungry beast that demands blood until there is none left to have and its allies work to foster chaos and plant the fertile seeds of distrust and hate. It is said by some that there were whispers that came in the darkness of night, whispers that came as dreams to those sleeping Kings who had raised their armies and swung their swords, whispers that sowed the seeds of this conflict and told them lies that they were going to be invaded and conquered. Whispers that came from the dark witch Lady Hush and her servants and which gave birth to that demon called War. This was a time in the lands when war was a very common thing. These wars were small affairs with little bloodshed and their conflicts ended in days when both sides lost interest in fighting but there was something different at work this time. This was not one of the temper tantrums of old, this was a full-scale assault between lands that was fueled by the red magic of Hush, who poisoned the minds of all that took up a sword, cursing them to fight and keep fighting until they could no longer pick up the smallest dagger. The war spread like a disease and it infected all who touched a sword and the conflict grew and grew until it was only the Kingdom of Man that refused to choose a side or fight.

The Kingdom of Man was under the rule of the second Mistress of Magic at the time of this grand conflict and even as her borders were crossed by warring armies she swore not to take part in the affair. Even as her subjects called for a response she refused, Lady Leearr swore not to spill blood unless she had no choice. Too much blood had been shed, too much fear had been sown, and she would not add to the madness. The Mistresses were still a new idea in the Kingdom and she was looked at with distrust by her own people and the people outside of her borders. She was uncertain what to do but trusted in her instinct, and in the visions she had of the Mother Wood which told her that war was no way forward. She refused to let her people fight so instead she had the first borders installed by the people of the Kingdom, built when the people would rather tend their farms and homes and lives. Fences were built with whatever was available to the area, stones, trees, dirt, anything that would work. In some places they were several feet high but in many places the fences were barely begun and so shabbily built that they barely stood against the elements before they started to crumble. The Kingdom had released all but a small group of soldiers and these soldiers that may have protected the Kingdom instead were sent out to help build the borders but it was poor and piecemeal work for most of these men and women were not masons and knew nothing of building walls and did little to protect the Queen's people. The Queen, as wise as she was, was ignorant to the real tolls of war and the dangerous costs of peace. Simple walls were not enough, and with her diplomats recalled there was nothing to do but wait and see what came next and the people despite their uneasiness still trusted their Queen, their Mistress, but gathered any weapons or items of magic they could just in case. Once the smoke got so thick that the skies became black and the animals disappeared the work on the walls ceased and the people turned their eyes to the forests and borders and waited. With most walls unfinished and no standing army to stop them the soldiers of the other lands marched through the Kingdom of Man unabated. These soldiers were not supposed to be passing through the land but no one tried to stop them and so the armies marched through peacefully, not even engaging one another when they encountered each other but respecting the uninvolved nation enough to save their fighting until they made it back across the border again. This was not what had been promised to the Queen but there was little she felt she could do without endangering her people so she kept to her Seeing Stones and had her guard disperse into the towns and villages to keep an eye on things and that was all. It wasn't what was promised but there was peace and sometimes that is the best thing you can hope to have.

So the Queen waited, and watched, and hoped that this storm would soon blow over like the past had.

This peace would not last.

It was near to the Harvest Festival and the Reaping when the war finally took its toll on the Kingdom of Man. A young farmer had left his wife as she slept to go out to the far edges of their land to check on their pumpkin crop. The crop was going to put more money in their purse than they had ever had in the five years they had been working the land. Enough money, maybe, *maybe* to finally fill the nursery he had been secretly planning as he worked day after day. These thoughts of his beautiful wife, and the children to come were the thoughts that followed the man as he looked over the pumpkins and ran his calloused hands over their skins, his smile wide, and joyful, and as bright as the sun. As he looked over the crop it was the smell of smoke that woke him from his daydreaming and as he rose and turned towards where the smell was coming from he caught the sight of a great fire off in the hills in the neighboring land and a vast, thick wall of black that hung and roiled along the border. The man stood slowly as there seemed to be movement in that cloud and he cursed himself for never working to build the wall there better or higher when suddenly he saw a group of men emerge from the darkness and climb over the low stone wall and begin making their way across the edge of his neighbor's land and then his own. The farmer cursed and spat as he watched all this. He was not a fighter, never had been and had no interest in becoming one which was what had drawn his wife to him in the first place – his compassion outweighed his rage – but this, this was an outrage. These men, these soldiers, these burners were walking brazenly across the land of his neighbor and were now on his land and crossing towards him without so much as a wave or gesture to show they meant him no harm. Maybe this was their way where they were from but here that was not what one did. The farmer had worked his hands until they bled to earn this land and when he had earned it he worked even harder to make it what it was now. This was *their* land. The farmer was not a fighter but he was no fool and with the war had come things from the deeps of the forests that were not meant for sunlight and were no friend of Man, things which the wars had awakened and which meant to do nothing but harm and spread nothing but death. These were dangerous times so he carried a Sunstone which his wife had given him, a thing of magic that, when brought into full sunlight, would light up and blind, sometimes temporarily, sometimes permanently, those foolish enough to look into its depths as it exploded. The farmer thought about the stone that lay sleeping in his pocket and that if these men meant him trouble they would surely regret coming here with no invitation.

"Hail, men from afar. What brings you through my land this morning?"

The farmer waved his right hand at the band of strangers and smiled while his left hand rolled the Sunstone over and over and over in his pocket. Waiting to see what their response would be.

"Farmer, make way, we have no time or interest in your simple banter and or gestures. We mean to walk through this land and you stand in our way. That is a mistake. Move aside or fall before us." The strangers were getting close enough that the man could make them out now and he saw that the one who spoke was younger than himself which meant he was at the edges of his teen years yet he lead a force of twenty men. Curious. So who was he? A prince? No, hardly. Then what was he? The farmer bit his lower lip and heard the voice of his wife in his head telling him to step aside and to let them pass but the farmer would not yield. This was their land. He may let them walk through but they would at least give him the respect of going around him. They would do that at the least. As he stiffened his stance though he thought again of his wife and of the unfinished nursery and a future yet to be written and he dropped his head, released the Sunstone and let it fall into the deeps of his pocket and stepped aside. This was not worth dying for and he had a feeling that these were men who shed no tears over murder. The invaders halted their progress a short distance from the farmer and talked among themselves before their leader made a motion with his hands and then they all began moving forward towards the farmer and fell into a single file line as they altered their path a little so that they passed the farmer to his right and moved onward. He listened to them walking away until he could hear them no longer and then he raised his head and turned to see where they had gone. His mouth fell agape when he saw that they were not far at all, standing in a group just past him near the stand of trees where he would eat his lunches each day he was in the field. The men stood silently watching the farmer, faint grins carved into their stern faces. As they saw his sudden shock and watched him take a stumbling step back they all began laughing raucously. The one who had spoken, the one who lead them here let them laugh for a moment before raising an arm, which stopped them all immediately. The leader of the men was looking at the farmer and smiling darkly for a moment before spitting at the feet of the man before him, his smile fading and a deep frown setting itself into his face.

"How dare you. How DARE you act so prideful, farmer. Do you know that this land is rightfully my mother's? Did you know that? No, of course you didn't. Because your people don't know your history. You only know the history that is told to you, or sung to you, or which you make up. You don't own this land.

You have no claim here. None of your people have any claim. By rights *all* of this should be my mother's. It was she that sowed the first seeds here, and she that brought the things up from the ground and gave birth to the first trees and stones. She even let your kind live when you crawled out of her spit. Do you understand me, farmer? Do you understand what I am telling you?" The young man's rage aged him and his eyes seemed to glow faintly. The farmer took another step away from him.

"Is your mother the Queen then? Is that what you are saying? I did not know the Queen had a son your age."

"*Queen?* How dare you? How *dare* you? She is not a mere Queen of these lands but the Mother, the mother of this place and the place beyond the trees. She is the Queen of *all* lands."

"My apologies. I guess I don't know who she

is. Truly I can say I have never heard of your mother or of her claim on my land. Unfortunately I purchased this property from the House of the Lands so if you feel you have a claim here I would direct you to them, not me. By the way, may I ask how it is then that a Prince of all lands would come to live in one of the nations that are at war?"

At this the strange young man laughed.

"No, farmer, no, I am no Prince. I am nothing as lowly as that. And as for home, we claim no land as home. *All* lands are our homes because all of them are ours; we are merely letting your kind tend to the grounds before we take back ownership. Farmer we are a passing wind, an ill wind if it pleases you, with fire on our heels and carrying purses filled with dust and we are coming from the grave and we are headed to the land to your North. We had no interest in you farmer until I saw the arrogance in your face and then, oh then we thought we would come to play."

The nastiness in the smile made the farmer take another step back.

"Arrogance? What arrogance? Sir, I am sorry if you took my desire to know who the strangers are that tread my lands but I had meant it as no disrespect. If you mean to pass through then please do so and move on and leave me and my land alone. I have no time for games so please, I ask you again, move on. " The farmer's rage was suddenly renewed, pushing itself to the surface, forcing its way up but he held it in check and latched onto his wife's calming voice as he reached deep into his pocket and grabbed the Sunstone.

"Oh but good farmer you have been so kind to us we want to repay you with a game. I want to show you a game. It's an old game, a game my mother taught me when I was still very young. This is an old game, one I am sure you have seen others play over the years but you have never played it, have you? No, I think not. And you certainly never thought you would play this game at such a youthful age yourself but, well, we're here to change that. So let's play a game, farmer. This game is called Death."

The young man turned from the farmer and as he turned there was darkness about his face. He took pleasure in this but it was a kind of pleasure the farmer could never and would never understand. He took several more steps backward and tried to pull the stone free but each time he tried the stone slipped out of his hand. Run. He had to run. Run and hope he could make it to cover or over the fence and lose them. It was his only hope. Before he could make a step though the stranger move his hands together and heard him say something he couldn't make out and then a sudden and stinging pain shot through him. The stranger turned to face the farmer and his face was inhuman, was a thing carved from wood and bone with eyes too deep and a mouth like that of a rotten jack of the pumpkins and thick gray things like roots made of bone that sprouted from the man's arms and legs. It was all too much and the farmer wanted to scream to scream to scream and run as fast and as far as he could but he knew it was too late. It was just too late. The farmer felt his skin itching, felt as if he was covered in burning worms, felt his thoughts turn molten, and felt the sweat that covered him become scorching rivers. The farmer opened his mouth and all that came out was fire, fire that burst from his eyes, his ears, from every pore of his body and in an instant the world fell away and all went black, then all went white and the farmer flailed to put himself out but found he was only spreading the fire and in another moment he was covered. A million things raced through his mind. He thought of his wife and screamed out for her, for the life they were meant to have and flames shot high into the air. The farmer pushed his hand deep into his disintegrating pocket and grabbed the sun stone, wanting nothing but to make these monsters pay for what they had done but it was too late and his pockets were gone, pants were gone, all was gone and everything turned the color gold and when his heart finally broke he was overcome with a mountain of grief but then it left and in its place was a feeling of complete and utter peace and he smiled with his molten mouth as he saw, out beyond the invaders a beautiful woman that was lit with a soft blue and he knew it was the first Mistress of Magic and that he would hurt no more and his smile widened and widened and widened until there was nothing left of him and then he was gone and in his place there was a crooked scarecrow wearing his clothes. The raiding party watched silently as the farmer burned, died, and then changed, watched as he became the scarecrow, watched with humorless grins that hid their secret terror that someday, some day that might be one of them turned into something else, something terrible should they ever anger their master. The party turned their weary eyes to their leader and watched as his hideous form changed back to that of a tall, wiry man and each of them shivered to see it. The Son watched the farmer silently and when the transformation was complete he strode up to the scarecrow and spat at its feet and the ground around the area, the pumpkins, the weeds, and everything that grew all around turned to ash as far as the eye could see. The Son moved closer to the scarecrow and lifted a thin hand and ran it across the burlap face. He leaned in close and whispered something into where the ear would have been and the scarecrow let out a long, loud sigh and it shifted in the earth as its shoulders slumped and then it was still again. The Son turned away from his work and back to his raiders –

"We are done here. The fire beckons. It's time to leave."

With that he walked between his men and away towards the horizon and they quickly followed and it was silence that leads them and fire that followed and it wasn't long until the sky was full of ash.

Away in her home the young wife knew nothing of what had transpired out in the fields nor of her husband's fate. No, the wife simply sang the old songs; the songs of her people as she sharpened the kitchen tools, put a stew on the stove, and read one of her mother's books. As the hours passed and the day danced into the shadows the woman began to get worried when her husband didn't return and scared when he didn't return by nightfall. This was not like him. Not at all. Something was wrong. She looked out the kitchen window and toward the fields and way off in the distance she saw the red glow of war and her fear became an ever tightening knot in her chest. Something. Was. Wrong. Her heart was racing and her thoughts were out of control so she remembered the words of her father - *breathe and all will come clear.* She took a deep breath, then another, then another and she closed her eyes and focused her mind and instead of her husband she saw a face she didn't recognize. A face harsh and full of angles - a mask hiding something else, something terrible. She opened her eyes and felt something twist in her. She had had visions like that before, something passed down from her father, and they never meant anything good. Something was very, very wrong. She had to find him; she had to find him...and now.

The young woman left their home with neither shoes nor shawl and walked out towards the fields where her husband would have gone and where she felt he was now and with each step she moved a little faster and a little faster and before she knew it she was running out to him. The ground was cold on her bare feet but the face of the stranger burned bright behind her eyes and drove her on. The world of night was a blur as she ran and she concentrated on her husband and only slowed as she neared a figure standing just ahead of her but when her feet touched the warm ash that covered the ground she knew something horrible had happened and suddenly knew that her husband was dead. Their fields, their beautiful fields that her love had sworn would one day be the land they would hand down to their children and they to their children and on and on and on was gone, all of it was gone, all of it burned to nothing. Ruined. Rotten. The fields her husband had worked until his hands were torn and bloodied were gone withered and dead and at the center was a mound of ash and beside it there stood a scarecrow hanging limp and still from its wooden supports. The woman recognized the clothing on the scarecrow immediately as those of her husband's and let out a scream and ran to it and grabbed its head in her hands and held it up so she could look into its featureless burlap face. Perhaps, perhaps... There was nothing to see there but two black buttons sewn to scorched cloth but she could feel him, could feel the last of him inside of it, the last of his fire as it cooled and knew this was her husband. She knew this was him and that everything they had dreamed and hoped was now gone and something in her broke and blackness started to fill her. She closed her eyes all she saw was black but a living black that was awake and ravenous but she tried to push it back, to focus on the world around her and as she did she felt something cool beneath her foot and looked down and there was the thick silver band her husband had worn since they had promised one to the other and beside it was the stone she had given him for protection. She fell to her knees and howled with rage and sorrow and felt the blackness in her pushing outward. She dug her hands into the ash and screamed and screamed and screamed, the blackness filling her to overflowing and whispering to her as she screamed. The scream rose higher and higher until the ground cracked around her, the dead trees shook, the scarecrow shifted and fell over, and in the distance the fence crumbled. The widow looked up from her grief and sniffed the air and smelled smoke and fire and smelled *him,* the one that had done this. She screamed and her head filled with words, with speaking, with curses and suddenly the dark spells came to her, the things she was taught by her older sisters, the things taught to her but which her mother had forbidden her to ever use but her family was far, far away now and she was alone, all alone and there was no one to stop her. The blackness within her latched onto these spells and held them aloft in white flames to her and everything became clear. There was nothing left. Nothing left but revenge. She smiled and was transformed, her exotic beauty gone and replaced with a savage wildness that her husband had never known. A wildness none had known save her own kind, the water people who had learned the ways of things once forgotten by the people of the land. Things they had discovered and learned anew to protect their lands from those that might invade but she had sworn never to use the dark ways when she met the man who would become her husband but she cast aside any childish promises and knew only one thing – *revenge*. She drove her hands into the ground and grabbed up fistfuls of the ash and held it up to the sky and said two words before she poured the dirt down her throat, choking on it but swallowing as much as she could and what she couldn't she smeared over her face. Once this was done she leaned forward and whispered into her closed fists – *as my love undone, so thee undo* – retched the ash out into a thick, black mass on the ground. She put a filthy hand into her long curls and pulled out a handful and thrust it into the wet ash then pulled a small white stone from her pocket and put that into the center of it all and leaned forward so her tears would mix in as well. When she was done she leaned back and said three words silently and the mass began to bubble and pulse and then to smoke and she scooped it up and held it in her hand and felt its growing heat. She slowly rose and turned to face the long expanse of woods where she had smelled her enemy. He was at rest with his men, laughing at the fool in the field as they ate a hearty dinner. She smiled a smile no one would want to see and live, a smile of the servant of the grave, and she lifted her blew on the thing within and then held her hands aloft and out of the mass erupted two long black wings, a small black head and then the rest of a bird that looked too large to have been within the mass she held. It raised its wings and flapped them and with every flap they lit up red, bright and brilliant and growing darker and more fierce with each flap and within a few beats it was up and away and with every flap it grew redder and redder and nearer and nearer the widow's enemy until it was a flaming arrow of her vengeance that trailed fire in the sky. She watched with narrowed eyes and her hands balled into fists as her emissary made its way toward her enemy and in a few moments there was a single scream that became the scream of many and the night went from black to red as the forest exploded into an inferno. She felt him writhing, screaming, and running as his men died helpless around him. She felt the skin of the man fall off and the thing beneath was revealed and it was hurt, yes, it was hurt and badly. It screamed for its mother who didn't answer and it began tearing at the burning floor of the forest, digging until its clawed hands were red like the fire that coursed over its body, digging until it had dug deep enough to bury itself and escape the flames and after a long while it was still and fell into a deep blackness which the widow could not penetrate. Perhaps it was death. Perhaps it was simply a sleep like death. Whatever it was the beast was not likely to awaken from it. The widow let out a low laugh and turned away from the flames.

Enough.

She had enough of this war, this place, and this world and its hatred.

She had had enough.

She bent down and lifted her scarecrow husband and planted it back into the ground and then tipped its head back and kissed it gently on the lips. And then it came - The flood. She had been able to hold the torrents back while she did her work but now that it was over she was suddenly flooded with so much pain and so much sorrow that it doubled her over. She had loved this man so much, had dreamed of the family they would have, the life they would have and now it was gone, all of it gone. She howled and threw her hands to the sky and lightning lit up the night and as she cried she said one last spell and as she finished speaking she felt her feet become roots that burrowed into the earth. She threw her head back and screamed and her back bent and her arms stretched and twisted and her fingers became branches and from the branches blossom delicate black flowers that drip pure poison. Her body cracked and elongated and her face became bark and her mouth was frozen and then she was gone, her scream echoing along the hills and valleys as she stood silent and alone, a great tree forever beside her love but forever alone.

They say that this is a haunted place. A place forgotten in all the wars but known and avoided by the people. It is said that the sitting Queen comes and pays her private respects once every year to the Widow and the scarecrow that stands there still. And it is said that if a couple comes to her desperately in love they will know if their love is meant to be if the Widow weeps her black petals over them and gives them her sorrowful blessing.

Ah but this is but a story, a fable, a myth of a forgotten time that may best be left forgotten but I say that some stories are too true, are too painful, too sad, and are forgotten on purpose, and we are cursed to repeat them because we refuse to face them. I also say that not all stories are over once lived and once told and that this story may yet live on. This tale may not yet be fully told.

And so weeps the widow.

The Last Sheep

Part One

Son. Son. SON! Wake and listen well. You have slept too deeply and too long and the world has begun to pass you by. It is time to awaken. Awaken and take what is rightfully yours. Do you hear it? Do you hear the sound of a thousand-million people marching on our enemies? Marching under your orders. Marching with arms of fire and voices of ash and you leading them into the Thicket and towards revenge. It is time to wake up and to get revenge for what they did to me. It's time. WAKE UP!

The Son woke from the sour dream and grimaced as he rubbed a gnarled and scarred hand over his ruined face. Where was he? All around him was dirt and darkness and the faint scent of fire. Where... Oh yes, buried. Burned. Someone had hurt him; someone had hurt him and killed his men. Someone had taken his face and sent him cowering into this dark place. When was that? He wasn't sure but it felt like a distant nightmare. It was long ago. So long ago. He wanted to go back to sleep, to sleep forever but he knew that that voice he had heard, the face he had seen wouldn't let him. It was time to wake up. It was time to rise and return to the world. It was time to make the world suffer.

Mother was calling and her words were like flames. The Son uncurled his aching hands and began to dig himself free.

X

The Thicket was angry.

For countless years Ashley Pickles had stood guard over what many believed was the most dangerous part of all the Kingdoms – the last wild and untamed land. A land that refused to be tamed. Ash had come here to stand guard because it was his calling. It was his duty. It was his honor. Once upon a time Ashley had been a lost young man searching for meaning in a big world that he felt he was but a small piece of a big, big world. He had found himself, his voice, in music and had thought that he was meant to be the center of all and had let himself be lead astray and had become lost again, lost until he found this place. Here, at the edge of the Thicket, he had found that there are no small pieces, that every leaf, branch and twig makes up the forest of the world and that all of it is necessary to maintain balance. All of it works together in concert to survive. It was a wild place, a temperamental place but it was beautiful. Here he had found his home, his peace, and friends that made sure he was never alone. And such friends they were. There were the Bumble Kitties who lived in the trees and who would join him in his music and songs. There were the Bloo Moos that would emerge from unseen holes in the Thicket to graze in the great valley below and whose milk cured any illness if you were fast enough to get it. There were the Pandas who would come to visit him on their way through the land to bring him provisions since he had become an honorary member of their tribe and sometimes they would tell him the news of the world. There were the Meep Sheeps who would come see him and would do air ballet for him when he was feeling down. And there was Queen Messy and her family. He didn't always see all of these friends often but these visits always reminded him *why* he was here and why he had stayed. There were some days when the clouds in his sky would return and he would think of the loved ones he had lost, his parents had moved out to a neighboring town to be closer to him before they had passed on to the Great Meadow. Many years earlier a woman had come from across the seas to hear him sing and having heard him stayed by his side until the day it was her time to go to the Meadow. He had lived a very long life and a very good life and there had been sadness but there had also been joy and it was the joy he would think most about when the clouds came back over the sun. It wasn't an easy life because he lived in the shadow of a living, breathing place that he had to protect from outsiders but at times must also protect the word against. Terrible things would try to sneak from the Thicket and into the world and while some managed to escape, with the help of the

Bumble Kitties Ash was able to scare these things back in most cases and slay those monsters that threatened harm to the world.

As dangerous as the Thicket was, as terrible as some of things within it were the Thicket was a barrier, a guard to something beyond it, far beyond it where few of any of the many tribes had ever gone. A place that the world was not yet ready to behold. A place with secrets Ash had dreamt about and heard whispers of in the shaking of the trees but which he knew he may never see. That he perhaps shouldn't see it. Ash knew that were the Thicket to fall and this place be revealed all the goodness in the world, all the dreams and hopes of all the tribes would wither away and die. It was this place that was the heart of the world, and that was what he really protected, that was the secret that he knew that so many others didn't. The Thicket was a dangerous place, this was true, a place where an old evil had been born and where its children still remained and was starting to rouse but beyond that, beyond the first tribe of Pandas, beyond the Bumble Trees, beyond the dark places where the Lady Hush first sowed her rage there was another place, a place where the lost were found, where the fallen rose, and where those at the end found their new beginning and that was what he protected. This place was made from the same things that made the universe and even Hush and the dark things had never dared to cross the threshold of this realm but the time was coming where nothing would remain sacred and even hope might fail. That was what Ashley had fought for and that was what worried him now because the Thicket was angry and he was an old man and his life's fire was starting to burn low. Near the Thicket age meant nothing as there were trees that were children of the stars and moons above and with the Bloo Moo milk Ash had fought illness, weakness, and even time but his watch was coming to a close and his time was running short. He could feel it. One way or another, his time here would be through and the thing that kept him up into the wee hours was a persistent question he couldn't quite shake – *who would come after him?*

A shadow was coming.

The Great Loneliness was waking, darkness long dormant was bubbling to the surface in the lands and off in the Citadel the age of Queen Messy was coming to an end. There was much that was changing and it was the end of an era and that was always a dangerous time. A time when the world could crack open and the Great Loneliness, that black enemy of all existence, would devour everything until no light remained. Ashley had seen these things in dreams and what he hadn't seen he had been told by Loof years earlier when he had come on his own one night. Ash now knew these things and he felt a growing terror because there were a great many things set on a collision course and however they worked out there would be blood, there would be death, and there would be one last war and there was nothing anyone could do to stop it.

Ashley heard a sound from behind him and didn't have to turn to know who it was.

"Is there anything you can do?" He asked.

"No. I don't know if any of us could at this point. It's gone too far. We held it off as long as we could have hoped. It was inevitable. Whatever happens next had to happen." The voice had a sad tone to it.

"Is it who we think it is? What we think it is?"

"Yes. Yes...and no. It's worse. So much

worse." And there was a long sigh from Mistress Anamare.

Ashley turned around but there was no one there. There was never anyone there, but he knew she had been there but was gone again, back into the Thicket. Back to where it began. Where everything began. And back to where all things would end.

X

She wasn't dreaming and she knew she wasn't dreaming. She had long since figured out the difference between her dreams and her waking life and this was no dream. It was real and so was the blood that was covering her hands. She was in Umwood forest again and he was digging dirt out of the ground in heavy clumps and as she dug deeper and deeper the dirt became mud and the mud slowly, slowly, slowly became something thicker and stickier. She knew she shouldn't be here at all, let alone by herself, that she shouldn't be digging, but she couldn't stop even as her hands burned with the pain of it. She was so deep into the ground that she was surrounded by earth and it was more liquid than solid anymore and then suddenly everything beneath her fell away and all that remained was nothingness that seemed to go on forever. She floated there, hands limp and dripping into the darkness and unable to move when there was a sudden rush of hot air that carried a voice that said one word – *Mother.* She closed her eyes and when she opened them she was in the hole again and she dug her hands deep into the dirt walls and tried to pull herself up but couldn't find purchase. She dug them in deeper and felt roots and grabbed onto them but they pulled free and were suddenly bones - bones that glittered and glowed like the bones of Pandas were said to glow. She spun around and dug her hands into the firmer dirt there and began climbing up, up, and out as cold air embraced her as she pulled herself free. She was exhausted, shaking and panting and wanting to be home. She was too weak to stand so she began to crawl slowly away from the hole and heard something roar beneath her and felt the ground shake and then watched as it cracked around her.

She was back.

She was back.

The monster was back and it was all her fault.

Beliar woke and was just able to stop herself from screaming by clamping her mouths over her mouth but could hear her heart pounding in her head and was covered in sweat.

A nightmare.

It was a nightmare.

Just a nightmare. She wasn't back at all. No, no, not at all. Beliar got up and ran through the dark to the bathing room and plunged her hands into the water and began scrubbing them with her eyes shut, not wanting to see if it had been more than a dream or not.

As Beliar did this in the room next door her sister Aribel wasn't able to stifle her own scream and it broke the silence of the Palace and rang through the night.

X

Things were changing and Messy hated it. The Queen hated change, and always had. Since she was a little girl she had struggled to find a balance between what she wanted to do and what she was supposed to do – who she wanted to be and who she was supposed to be and she still struggled with that and the more change there was the more doubt would flood in. Vix was her balance. He was her rock. He didn't mind change - Loved it, in fact. To him change was like a new land, an undiscovered kingdom, and every time you met a challenge and conquered it you became the King of that new land. To Vix, he was the King of a thousand lands and every day was the opportunity to discover another. And who was a better King than him? He let everyone have dessert at every meal because it was for them to decide what they needed and what was best sometimes – what other King would allow that? What other King trusted his Kingdom and his children enough to know that if you let people choose, if you trust them, they will surprise you more often than not by making the right choices because in the long run the right choices became the easiest ones to make. Messy admired that philosophy. Loved it. And loved him for it. But it scared her. It scared her because once upon a time she had chased only after change, chasing after the butterflies over the hill and then the sparrows over the next hill and on and on but then she became Queen and then a wife and then a mother and she slowly began to hate the notion of change and the tremors it brought.

With all the changes in her life the Queen changed as well. Gone was so much of what she had loved about herself, about her life, and with it was this overbearing responsibility and black fear of the unrest that lay at the edges of her land. Gone just as her King, her husband was for days, weeks, months on end as he traveled the lands to help keep the circle of peace unbroken, or gone across the waters to visit the land of his ancestors. Gone, leaving Messy alone to raise the girls, and alone to rule the Kingdom, and alone to face the darkness in her heart. Even the voices of the Queens of old were gone. The voices that had guided her, advised her, and consoled her in the bad times. Even those were gone. She could hear them, faintly, but not clearly. It was as if there was something blocking them.

These were bad times.

For years Messy had lived in secret fear, barely sleeping as she waited for Lady Hush to return and to rekindle the war. Waiting to hear her voice in her head and to for the ground to crack open to reveal her and her children. More than once she had heard the servants call her the Weeping Willow because of the haunted look in her eyes and obviously because they had heard her crying to herself during the long periods when Vix was gone. Ah, but they knew nothing of sorrow nor of weeping willows though she wondered if they knew she would often visit that lonely field and speak to the Willow there when times grew dark. Or if they knew that she often used a Seeing Stone to make sure that the Thicket was not on fire and that it still held back the darkness. And she wondered if they knew how deeply she feared war. The war. The last war. A last war to unite all of the nations under a red banner against the kingdoms that protected the Thicket. A war to burn the Thicket down to free the things within and to get at the mystery that lay beyond it. The last mystery. A last war to enslave, to murder, and to bring darkness into the lands again as it had been before the great Age of Understanding when the first Queen emerged. When she closed her eyes she saw fire and smelled smoke. But all was not dark in her heart. Her daughters were like twin suns, one that burned light and the other dark but both brilliant in their ways. And Vix, even in his absence left things for her to find, notes, gifts, reminders that even when he was away he was there with her. And she hated his absence, hated it to her core but understood that without his work away from the Kingdom and within the Kingdom that war may already have come. Both she and he had had to work very hard to remind the people that there may come clouds but there was always a warm sun behind them, waiting to break free. There was always hope. Though that hope seemed distant to her of late. She was becoming distant with Vix, Aribel, and Beliar and it hurt them, she saw it in their eyes but she was so afraid that something might happen to them, to all of them and that fear was deepening and it didn't help that dealings in her neighboring kingdoms could not be seen with the Seeing Stone – a safeguard spell that Loof had woven before giving her the gift. Even though much was shrouded from her she knew though that whether an arrow had been fired or not there was a war waging in her heart and she was losing. She had never realized it before but Lady Hush had poisoned her. Not with her deeds, not her words but her legacy, a legacy which had left a red trail that lead from the door of the Palace to the Thicket and through them to the Great Woods themselves. Since the death of Hush the Queen had learned of the horrible things the witch-woman had done and there were rumors that there were still those loyal to her in the Thicket, things that swore allegiance to her and which plotted against Messy and the Kingdom.

There was a wall in the heart of the Queen, a wall built brick by brick over the years and while she may try to blame a woman that had been dead and silent for decades she knew that she was the only one laying those bricks, and if she didn't find a way through that wall, she'd be trapped behind it forever.

X

Daughter. Daughter. DAUGHTER! It's time to return. It is time to crack wide this world and to loose the things of the darkness upon it. It is time to come back to me. AWAKE! Awake and show this world what you have learned in the Outer Black, return and tear the Thicket apart and pull free its beating heart. Free the Great Loneliness and let it bring eternal night to the world. Return my daughter, return and bathe in revenge.

The Daughter woke within the howling abyss and whimpered at the pain of life. Death had been quiet and cool but lonely. Too lonely. The Daughter woke and was surrounded by others like it, others that had been exiled into the vast emptiness and forgotten. It smiled as it felt its body awakening with a million points of pain and growled at the thought of inflicting a little of that pain on the one who had put it in this place and slowly began making its way home.

X

And suddenly the clouds began to thicken and the sun began to inch towards dusk.

X

"This…is…WAR!" Aribel screamed as she dropped her arm and gave the signal that set loose her army of Bumble Kitties.

Beliar howled with rage and turned to face her own brave warriors, a group of flop-eared Dizzer-Doos whose snouts wiggled in time with their stubby tails.

"ATTACK! No mercy!" Screamed Beliar.

The Dizzer-Doos all sat looking at Beliar, their large, single eyes fixed on the young woman with sudden curiosity.

"CHARGE!" Beliar yelled.

The Dizzers remained seated, still staring passively at the terribly loud human. One yawned and scratched itself and its eye started to close and its ears began to droop. A Bumble Kitty buzzed lazily over Beliar's head, one paw dipping into her thick dark hair as it headed for a Dizzer, which the kitty targeted then flew over in circle after circle.

The sisters looked at one another across the battlefield and snarled at one another.

This infraction demanded comeuppance!

This action demanded war.

The Dizzer looked up, targeted the kitty

and leapt high into the air, pushing off with its long arms and snatched the foe out of the air. Its prey well in hand the Dizzer landed safely and softly back on the bright green grass, its large, furred paws cushioning its landing and without any warning the Dizzer held the kitty out in front of it and a long blue tongue rolled out of its mouth and licked the face before it sloppily. The kitty gave a startled yelp and began batting its captor in the face with its paws, the Dizzer shaking with laughter as it did. Taking their cue, the other kitties rushed their enemies and tackled them and the Dizzers and Bumble Kitties all began to wrestle around on the ground in a mass of colorful fur. The kitties batted and the Dizzers licked and the air was filled with loud purring and short chuckles. Aribel dropped her head into her hands and Beliar shook her own head slowly from side to side and both sisters slowly made their way through the war to one another. Aribel looked at her sister with a crooked grin and shrugged as Beliar put a hand on her shoulder.

"So, uh, I win?" Aribel asked.

Beliar snorted with disgust and punched her sister in the arm.

"Well, I mean, I thought..." Said Aribel.

"Are there no better ways for two future Queens of the Kingdom of Man to spend their time away from studies than to play at war?"

It was Gloof, first son of the Great Loof and their personal guard and protector. Gloof knew the Queen and her family well and knew how close his father was to her and her kin so he had taken the job of protecting the girls freely and proudly, and it was a duty he took very seriously.

"You know Gloof you'd be a lot more fun if

you were, you know, more of a friend than a guard." Aribel replied with a grin.

"Ah, but that would imply that I liked you, wouldn't it?" Gloof replied.

Gloof was not as large and not nearly as serious as his father but to his foes he was dangerous. Gloof was much stronger than most of his tribe and much meaner when angered but he also had a deep affection for the Queen and her daughters, though it was the King and father who he was closest with. Gloof had become a confidante to the King and he considered this family as much a part of his tribe as any of his Panda brethren. The girls looked at their giant companion silently for a moment, unsure if the wiggling of his usually still ears meant he was joking or not but then Beliar, the more daring of the two sisters, let out a loud laugh and feigned a punch at Gloof.

"Oh, *you!*"

"I am joking, but only a bit. War is not a thing to play at, even with your furry friends. War is a dark thing, a grim calling that strangles all the good from the world. My father lost a brother to the old wars and I lost a sister in the border wars before you girls were born. Greed is the food of war and death the fuel for its machines. Play not at war, dear Princesses, rather, cherish life and cling to that light and spare your friend Gloof from a long lecture from the Queen." He ended with a smile but both girls felt the heaviness of his words and couldn't hold his gaze as he spoke, their embarrassment too great. Gloof frowned. He too had been a cub and had played at the same things when he was their age and he had never been told not to play at war but then he had had no choice then as war came to the Pandas whether they sought it or not. These girls deserved better. All the same he felt shame in having shamed them. He bent over and picked up a Bumble Kitty with one paw and a Dizzer Doo with the other and couldn't help but laugh as the two creatures batted playfully at one another.

"Though, I must admit Princesses, in all my days I dare say there has never been a war nearly as adorable as this one has been, though I would be loathe to choose sides, these are worthy, and cuddly adversaries. Now then, come, your father is back from across the sea and wishes to see you both."

"He's back?" Aribel squealed and spun away from her sister and Gloof and ran off down the hill towards the Palace, the kitties chasing after her. Beliar watched her sister disappear in the thick grasses then turned and looked at Gloof, and he could see the weight of many questions upon her brow. He let the quiet between them stand until she was ready to speak. He had learned from his father that a question will ask itself when it's ready. A question was not a bad tooth and must come free on its own.

Finally…

 "What do you know about dreams, Gloof?"

Gloof fell backwards on his haunches and sat heavily, stroking his chin and deep in thought. Beliar felt exposed now that the question was out there and she looked from the Panda to the boots on her feet, waiting for her answer.

 "Hmmm…We of the Panda Tribe take dreams very seriously. Your father would tell you that we take them *too* seriously but not your mother, no, she knows the power of some dreams, and the danger of them. Dreams are passageways into your inner self. Sometimes they are little more than diversions to keep you from worrying over the world too much, sometimes they are windows into your hearts true desires, but some dreams, some dreams are doors to dark places where you may fall under the power of things that want only for you to serve them. These dreams can be beautiful and dangerous things, like you humans but they can lead you astray and into the black parts of the Thicket. The parts you never escape from. Ah, but what your dreams mean, well, that's for you to decide. What I can say is that you must not force it, if you allow the dreams to tell you what they mean they will, just always remember that you control them, they do not control you. You must always be careful though child, the Kingdom of Dreams is the biggest of all the Kingdoms and ruled by a King and Queen, one who lives for mischief and the other for order and theirs is a very dangerous place to become lost so never stray too deep into dreams lest you lose your way back. But come, let us leave dark talk for brighter days and find the sunshine of your family and blow these clouds away."

Gloof held stood quickly and gracefully and held his paw out to the Princess, who looked up from her feet and into his blue eyes. Her face was shrouded with unanswered questions, the darkness that had always been within her boiling near the surface, but she forced a smiled and took his paw and the two of them began walking down the hill and towards her home.

X

The Great Loneliness was awake. It had been asleep for so long, for too long and it had been an uneasy sleep full of dreams of hate and revenge. A red sleep full of red dreams. But now it was awake. It was awake and it sensed something in the air.

Unease.

Distrust.

Change.

Curious to test the limits of its bondage the Great Loneliness stretched, spreading its roots out from the black tree it had been trapped within. It felt the roots tingle, twist and stretch outwards and as soon as they sank themselves into the pure soil of the Thicket the Great Loneliness grinned within itself, drunk with the taste. It had been eons since it had tasted freedom and it had forgotten how sweet it was. The Loneliness waited a moment, another, and then another and when there was no rebuff from the Thicket or its protective Druuns the Loneliness sent its roots farther and deeper and again nothing happened. It did this again and again and again until finally it realized that this entire part of the Thicket had been abandoned.

Abandoned!

The Great Loneliness straightened itself and rose tall once more, its body cracking loudly as it spread wide its branches and sunk deep its roots. A branch began to suddenly move, to twist, to bend, to become an arm full of dangerous barbs and the arm moved swiftly and slashed the trunk of the tree that was the Great Loneliness once and then twice and from those wounds came thick black fluid that pooled around at the tree's base.

It was time to shift the balance.

It was time to make the Thicket pay for the many years of hibernation the Loneliness had been forced into.

The black pool began to bubble from within it there was movement. Suddenly there was the sound of branches breaking and something large approaching and from the brush emerged a Druun, growling and lowering itself for attack. Roots erupted from the base of the tree and launched at the guardian but were batted away and severed with a thick, ornate spear worn smooth from years of use. The Druun grinned at its enemy and took a step towards the tree, then another, happy to hurt the Great Loneliness, to wound it so badly that it would never recover nor try this again but before it could take another step it was in the air in a confusion of motion. Thick vines wrapped around and around the guardian in a blur and all it could do was struggle feebly against its captor. More and more vines joined the others and there was nothing it could do and in a moment its spear fell into the thick mud and all was still again. The vines released the Druun and returned to the tree and as they did something began to crawl out of the black goo and then another thing, and another and another rose to join their master.

From behind the black tree there came a voice.

"So you have chosen to wake, is that so?" Spoke the stranger.

"No, I have chosen to take what should have been mine." The Great Loneliness replied.

"And what is it exactly that should have been yours?"

"*Everything!*"

The stranger came closer and looked the tree up and down before leaning forward to touch the dark trunk with its paw, lingering over the wounds. The tree hissed and the things from the muck roared but did not advance. The Panda looked up towards the higher branches of the tree and patted the trunk one last time before taking a step back and turning away to look at the rest of the Thicket.

"Well, then it seems we have a lot of work to do then, don't we?" Zum of the Thicket tribe replied.

X

"Sometimes I forget how beautiful it is here, away from the water." Vix told Messy and the girls as he stared out over the rolling orange of the Bember Hills.

"I suppose, if, you know, you like thick grasses, singing Tinder-Wallers, and the smell of flowers in the air then it's OK…" The Queen gave her a sideways smile at her husband.

"…And dear husband you know that these hills are always here for you when you return. Keep them not in your memory but in your heart and always in mind, lest you forget the sweet smell of home." Messy's playful tone unwound as she spoke and her smile faded as she looked beyond the Hills to the land far distant.

"Yes, yes, and I have kept it in mind and in heart but I have been long wondering...long wondering if this place wouldn't always be here for me to return to. If somehow it might simply...slip away."

The girls looked up from their sandwiches and at their father with identical looks of concern on their faces. They looked at one another and then to their mother, whose head was turned and her attention focused off down the hills. A picnic. A celebration. A time together without an envoy, without their entourage, and with just one another and now the clouds that had seemed ever present these last few years had returned. The Queen turned slowly back to her family and her eyes seemed distant a moment, looking at her family as if they were strangers. She forced a smile.

"Uh, wha? I'm sorry, I drifted off. I thought, I thought... " She started to drift again as she watched a Meep Sheep fly into and then out of a cloud but past it, on the far horizon she could have sworn there was black smoke rising.

Silence from Vix and the girls as words failed them.

Aribel broke the silence.

"What do you mean, dad? What do you mean it might slip away?"

"I mean that, well, I have been thinking that maybe, maybe it's time that the Carnival King's crown was passed down."

"WHAT?" Said the girls in unison.

"What are you talking about, Vix?" Messy asked, back now and not sure she heard her husband right.

"What I am saying is that I have held that crown for too long. I don't belong to that world anymore. I haven't for years. I haven't been needed across the sea in ages. I cannot live in two worlds and lose my connection to both. When the girls were born I went to the Blue Council and I proposed that a day may come when a successor must be chosen and so we began discussing things. It had become clear even to them that my heart was here, that my love was here, but since the land was not at war and the Carnival ran well without me it never became an issue. I knew that a time would come when they would ask me to return my crown and they knew that a time would come when I would be ready to move on and the time is now. I am ready. I should have known the very moment I looked into your mother's eyes, heck, maybe I did, but it took the absence of those eyes, and the absence of you girls to know for sure. The Carnival deserves an active King and this land needs...I need...I need to be here." Vix took Messy's hand and smiled at her.

"But *dad*!" Said Beliar.

Vix laughed and the clouds seemed to break.

"This isn't a bad thing. It's, well it's a wonderful thing. Life is full of change. Things *have* to change. Whether we like it or not, whether we fight it or go along with it they will always change. It's time for the Carnival Kingdom to change. Across the sea things are so, so different. The Kingdoms are so different but they, *we* learned from our wars, we learned and changed. The tribes to the North used machines, the tribes to the South used magic, and we were trapped between them and so many of us were lost. These were the days when my own father was a boy and the Carnival was in tatters, the Kingdom was in flames and our Song Fathers were dead. It was a little girl, my aunt that ended the war and changed our lands. And she was just a little girl."

Messy had never heard this, in all of their years Vix had never wanted to speak about the wars. She knew of them, from his father and others from his lands but he never wanted to speak of them. His family had lost many loved ones as the wars died down and it took a good long time for the smoke of war to clear, but it had. It had. But Messy never knew how and she had never met or even heard of an aunt. After a long pause Vix continued.

"The sky was black with smoke and the air was full of the moaning of the wounded. My father was lying unconscious in his bed, the

Queen was dead, and the King was deep in talks with his advisors as to what course to take. The Blue Lands are so much like this land, so very much, but the difference is that we had always been united because of the Song Fathers who joined our lands together in a way similar to what the Bumble Kitties do here. They calmed the raging tides of the heart and drove away the clouds that had covered so many minds. But they couldn't drive back all tides or all clouds. And I tell you girls that there are some things, some things that will never disappear no matter what we do and war is one of those things. We still must try though to make it a thing of memory and not instinct, a thing of reflection not reaction. When war returned to our lands it wasn't waged against a King or an ideal but was a war against all of us, and we were all family. It had been many years and the Blue Lands had united not under one flag but for one purpose. Our aversion to war and battle though lead some to think we were weak and so greedy eyes turned upon our many resources. Renegades from across the many nations banded together under a red flag and began attacking and the more they attacked and the more the Blue Lands pledged to defend but not attack the greater the numbers grew for the marauders. Within weeks things had gotten out of hand and the Lands were in chaos. Many of the carnivals fell victim to the renegades as they were seen as symbols of weakness that had infected the land and my family and especially my father were targeted specifically. If the Carnival fell then one of the last links to the Song Fathers would fall also and the land would lose hope and then the war."

Beliar interrupted.

"But why wouldn't they fight back? I don't understand…shouldn't you fight back?"

Vix gave her a weak smile.

"They did. They did. The people would defend themselves and had created defenses for their lands but after the last war there had been many weapons that had been cast aside because they were not just dangerous, not just deadly, but because to use them was to violate every law known to our kind. Those who we fought though knew only want and greed and used the most diabolical of devices and none could stand long before such weapons. It wasn't cowardice that allowed these people to destroy so much, to harm so many but fear for what might come next. So many fell. So many. Some parts of the Blue Lands will never be free of that poison. Some parts were walled off and all but forgotten. Some...well, but let me get back to the tale I was telling. Did I answer your question?" Vix ran a hand along Beliar's cheek.

"Yes." She said in a low voice, eyes still

focused on her boots as her cheeks flushed.

"Don't be embarrassed to ask about the past my dear, never, we can never learn from a thing, about a thing unless we first ask about it. There is still a question you haven't asked though that deserves an answer before I move on."

Silence met Vix for a moment until Messy's distant voice asked the question.

"Why?"

Vix leaned forward and grabbed and squeezed his wife's hand.

"Yes, why. Why? Why cause so much destruction, so much terror, and so much pain when things were good, or as good as they had ever been before? It's a question worth asking and one I didn't ask until I was a man myself but it's important. Why is always important because if you don't question why we do things, why *you* do things then you will begin to do anything and everything and lose yourself in the process. These people attacked because for some people the very act of being happy, of trying to be happy is like a declaration of war and for those people enough is never enough and some is never better than all and the need to destroy conquers everything else. Why did they wage this war against us? Because there was nothing else for them to do."

There was more heavy silence between the four of them and in the distance a bird screamed. Vix let the silence stand a moment longer then continued.

 "Back to the story at hand – Things had gotten dire. Our lands were not prepared for a war, especially not a war fought with such rage and things were getting very bad. My aunt had watched helplessly as those around her, as the people dearest to her fell in battle and she was heart-broken to have nothing to offer as aid. She felt helpless. One morning she awoke though and told those around her that she knew what she had to do and she went immediately to the Summoning Stone that was in the very center of the Kingdom. The Summoning Stone had been used in ceremonies for hundreds of years but was now overgrown with weeds. Whatever had happened as she slept it lead her back to this sacred place where she performed the ancient ceremony to call forth the Grunk."

"What exactly was the Grunk?" Asked Aribel.

"The Grunk was an ancient thing that had come from the time before time, a remnant of the sky tribes that ruled ages before. It was a thing they had made, from magic and from land, and it lived for one thing and that was to destroy. The sky tribes lost control of the

Grunks and there was a great battle that put an end to the reign of that tribe but also put an end to the Grunks. This Grunk was the last of them. The rest had gone into the sea, or the stars, or just between the folds of the world and had disappeared as the sky tribe had. When the beast had wandered the land and sea destroying everything in its path the Song Fathers had sung it to sleep and had trapped it within the folds of the land. The Song Fathers had not wanted to destroy the beast because they felt it was not theirs to destroy life but also because a day might yet come when such force was needed so they wove a spell to hold the Grunk and forged a capstone to cover where it slept. Should a day arise when it was needed the Summoning Stone would be there to release it. I like to think that the Song Fathers had hoped the Grunk might be set free so it could return to its people one day. My aunt had spent hours and hours in the library and had learned many of the rituals and customs of the lost tribes and so she knew what it took to summon the Grunk and what it would do when it awoke. The Grunk was powerful, more powerful than most could imagine and in order for it to rise it took precious life to awaken it and when it returned it would do the bidding of the one who awoke it but then it would be uncontrollable and burn everything before it to ash."

"She..." Messy asked, from a thousand miles away.

"She risked everything and sacrificed everything in order to call forth this monster. And when the peoples of the Blue Lands and the renegades all saw the horror that rose from the earth, saw a thing that all knew by name and knew the terror it would spread there was no choice but to join together to fight it or they would all lose everything. It was only by fighting a common enemy was the war against one another ended. You see, even in the midst of the madness there was the last breath of sense and it was that sense that joined the warring sides and their armies together and with great cost to all sides the Grunk was sent into the darkness beyond the worlds, not into death but into the place beyond. When it was over, when the fires began to die and the smoke to clear all the hate had left the hearts of the people and after that the warring peoples all returned to their Kingdoms and for many years there was nothing said between the lands until one glorious Mid-Summer Day the Carnival King and his Carnival returned and when it returned so did the people, and so did the world. People had seen the worst, had survived it, and for all but a few the taste of war had gone sour. Which is not to say there were no more fights, or skirmishes, or disagreements but that people knew the danger of going too far, of pushing too hard and that was the change. It wasn't the threat of a more diabolical weapon that changed people but the realization of all that has been lost and could have been lost if we didn't stop on the path we were on. War begets war. Hate begets hate. And if you live to destroy then a day will come when someone or something much more powerful sets its sights on you. A change had come, the sort that this land has never seen. It has seen terrible things, it has seen Lady Hush but it has never seen something that shook it so hard that it shook the people free of their need for war."

"But dad people didn't just...stop, I can't believe that." Said Beliar.

"They didn't. Not for a long time. There was fighting, as I said, but so much had been lost, so many had been lost that the sorrow was deeper than any hate and before that hate could flourish again the Carnival returned to remind people that there was more to life, more to *us* than that. That we were united in our dreams and our joy. But it took a catastrophic change for that to happen."

This was something Messy had never thought of and a horrible thought occurred to her that she kept to herself – had they really done the best thing when she had stopped Hush when they had? Was it possible they should have let her...No. *No.* She realized she was looking off again towards the distance where it looked like the sky was darkening.

"And honestly they need someone that will be there, that can advise the Kingdoms and can guide the Blue Lands. I can't be that person. I have tried but I can't. I belong here now. This is my home. After much discussion, after much planning and plotting we have made a plan to find my successor so I can finally step aside."

"But who?" The three asked at once, which made Vix laugh, and when he laughed all three did, which lightened the mood considerably.

"Do you remember Messy, a young boy from this land that would sing for all the people? A boy that had a voice like and angel? I believe our friend Ashley had inspired him."

"Yes, yes I do, his name was Glen. I am not sure if you kept up with him or not but he a few years ago he stopped singing, stopped speaking, and stopped everything as a matter of fact."

"Why would he do that, dad? Gloof used to take us to hear him when he came. It's been a while, we were still little girls but he has a beautiful voice. Why ever would he stop?" Asked Aribel.

"I think he learned a lesson Mr. Pickles had

learned many years before and that your mother may be very familiar with - Sometimes when people want something from you and want that thing and only that thing it weighs on you and turns you sour towards that gift you once loved. I believe that's what happened to him. I know that one day during a performance he just stopped singing and walked off the stage and that was that. He refused to speak to speak to anyone and hid away in his home and after a while people just left him alone. I went to see him a few months ago, unsure what I would find and not really sure what I was looking for but I went just the same. I went out to his home, which was still well maintained with a wonderful little garden and I introduced myself to him as he sat on his porch swing. I asked if I might sit with him and he shrugged his shoulders and so I thanked him and sat on his porch stairs. I never bothered him, simply sat with him and watched the world pass and then thanked him for his time and left. After that every few days I would go out and sit with him and sometimes I would read and other times I would look over some papers regarding the Kingdom but usually I would just watch the sky. One particularly hot day he asked me if I'd like some lemonade and I told him I would be much obliged for a glass and when he came back we started talking about and began to talk about gardening. Slowly, very slowly he became Glen again and we would talk about ourselves, and he told me he had known my wife many years earlier and that he too had come from across the sea and we realized we had a great many things in common. When one day he finally sang for me, a song from our home land I knew I was right in seeking him out. I was right about him."

"What were you right about, honey?" Messy asked.

Vix leaned back and smiled, pushing his arms further behind him and letting his hands sink into the thick, soft grass. He let the moment linger as it had when he first heard Glen sing. He focused on the wind in his hair, the sound of the Butter-Bugs and off in the distance the sound of a Meep Sheep 'meeping' in the distance. He turned his attention back to his family and his smile grew even wider.

"I was right that he was a Song Father."

"A *what*?" Asked all three.

"A Song Father. I come from, I mean, my *family* comes from Song Fathers, and my grandmother was a Song Mother. But along the way we focused more on the Carnival and less on the songs and we thought the line died out. My great-great-great family members had discovered that with certain magic they could bring their songs to life in ways that words and music alone couldn't and that was how the first Carnival was born. In no time my people focused more and more of their attention on what they could do with the Carnival and slowly they begin to forget the Old Songs and how to make songcraft and that sort of magic. For years we thought the Song Fathers were all gone when we had one here all this time. Glen's family comes from the Blue Lands, like me, and his family was once part of the Carnival Kingdom, our wonderful roaming nation."

"Then you're, but how, I..." Aribel asked.

"Yes, somehow, in some distant way we are related, which is why we're both so very dashing at our advanced ages. Not as dashing as the Queen but then how can one compare to a Mistress of Magic?" Vix looked at Messy and saw the worry in her eyes, the worry of things far away and he smiled at her and that worry melted, just a little.

He continued.

"But I am rambling, look, the sun is almost gone now and the Meep Sheep are leaving the skies for their homes in the deep grass, brother moon is getting ready to wake, and the chill is rising in the air. It's time to wrap this long tale up. After I heard Glen sing I asked if he had ever heard of the Song Fathers and he told me he had but that they were gone. I smiled at him then and patted his leg, by this point we were both sitting on the swing, and I told him they weren't gone yet. We talked a little more and I convinced him to go back to the old land to speak to some people who agreed with me and so, for the first time in more than a hundred years a Song Father has become the King of the Carnival."

"So he stayed?" Messy asked. He

remembered Glen as a boy still, and how beautiful his voice was. His voice like touching the sweetest of dreams to hear him. How was it possible, so much time passing? She still felt like a girl, like the confused teenager unsure what path to take in her life. She looked at her own daughters and realized that it was their turn to make those very decisions and she didn't envy them that one bit.

"Yes, he's the new Carnival King and, well, I am just regular old King Vix of the Kingdom of Man again. I will serve as an advisor and am here if something happens and they need me but essentially my time with the Carnival has passed."

"Aren't you sad?" Aribel asked.

"No. I knew for a long time that my heart wasn't in it anymore. I just can't be in two places at once and felt as if I was in neither place ever. I will miss the Carnival but I can always visit. *We* can always visit. My place is here though."

Vix looked at the girls and grinned at them and gave them a wink. Vix rose and ruffled his daughters' heads and looked over at Messy and her eyes were clouded, this time clouded because of him. He had expected this and had dreaded it. He hadn't told her any of this, not out of a need to be secretive but out of a need to keep any unneeded stress from her shoulders. He had loved Messy from the very moment he had seen her, had fallen into her eyes and been her's forever but her anger, though it was slow to rise, was something he was never anxious to roust. There was something happening in the Kingdom, a dark wind blowing, and he knew her mind was on that and he didn't want to cloud her already full mind with things that she needn't worry over.

"Well girls, it looks like Master Charles is here to take you back in to get you ready for dinner so you two head inside and your mother and I will join you in a few minutes. Deal?"

The girls knew their mother's anger and knew more than their father that it wasn't as slow to rise as it used to be and took more time to fade and they were loathe to leave their father but knew they must. Suddenly Messy and Vix were alone as the sun turned red.

"And not once in all this time did you think to tell me? To even talk to me about this?" She was mad. Madder than he'd seen her in ages. Mad enough to know that she was holding back. Angry enough that the rainbow of her hair had become black.

"I never told you because I knew you'd be upset. And I knew you'd be angry when I didn't tell you." Vix couldn't take his eyes off of her hair. It reminded him of Ariel's but her face, how set and angry it was reminded him of Beliar.

"How *dare* you? How dare you hide this from me? I never, I *never* wanted you to choose me over your home, never." Her hair was back to its normal colors, though with a gray undertone, and he could hear tears in her voice.

"It was my choice to make and I chose my present, my future, my *family* over my past. That is not my place any longer and to act as if it was would be to live a double lie. It was hard, harder than I care to admit but it had to be done. They need a King and I need to be here. And if you want the honest truth, the full truth - I never told you because I know you know she's back."

The light was almost gone from the day but he could see well enough to see that Messy's mouth fell open at this.

"You, wha, wha, *you what*?"

"Messy, honey, I know she's back. And I know you know it too. I don't have the gifts you and the girls do but I do have some things handed down to me from my family and I know she is back. Somehow, some way, she is back. And with her comes darkness. I have seen it in your eyes since the first rumors that there was unrest at the borders again. It started with arguments between farmers from our Kingdom and the others, then it became fights, then a few farms burned, and now there is talk of black smoke in the distance and rumors that the Black Machines are being forged again. There is only one person that can inspire this talk. One person that can set this land on fire again. That's what you were looking for tonight, wasn't it, the smoke?"

"Yes, I was looking for the smoke of the machines." Messy whispered, eyes straying to the horizon again.

"So was I, and there was none. Whatever is going to happen hasn't happened yet. There's still time."

"Oh Vix, can it be true? Can all of this be happening again? I thought she was gone. I thought it was over."

"Messy it wasn't over, not yet. An evil like hers, hatred like hers just doesn't disappear, it inspires. There were rumors years ago of a thing that was hiding in Umwood, a vile, dangerous monster that was poisoning the woods and killing the animals there but all of a sudden it seemed to disappear as did all talk of it. It was strange because I had asked Arnk about it at the time and he refused to speak of it, insisting there was nothing foul there, though I knew he was lying. I didn't press him but something happened out there and he knows what it was. Honey, something has been at work here, in these lands, since before any of us were born. Something nasty and vile. It's always been put off and avoided but it's time we face it. And we're going to face it together. All of us. Because there may be terrible things in this world but to every cloud there is a Meep Sheep. There is always hope. Always." He smiled at her.

 Messy looked at her husband, finally realizing how much he had sacrificed for her, for the girls, for the Kingdom, and she fell into his arms, her anger gone. He kissed the top of her head then held her away from him and kissed her forehead, then looked into her big eyes a moment before kissing her mouth softly.

 "You know, in all your story telling and showing off, King Vix, you forgot what day this is, didn't you?" Messy said into his chest through sniffles.

"Gosh, oh, wait; let me see, what *is* today..." Vix replied, happy to see that his surprise hadn't been ruined yet.

Suddenly there were screams from inside the Palace.

"AHHHHHH! DADDY! AHHHHH! CAAAAAAAAANNNNNDDDDDDYYYYYY" The girls cried out in unison as they saw the sweets he had brought from his travels. Sweets not found in this or any kingdom but the Carnival Kingdom.

"Oh, you are a sly one, my King." Messy looked up at Vix and smiled.

"How could I forget All Hearts Day when I have three beautiful women who I owe my heart to?"

"So sly..." Messy went on her tiptoes and

kissed him, stroking his face as she did.

Vix pulled away from Messy and pulled something from his pants pocket, brought it to his lips and kissed it, then put it quickly over his Queen's head and around her neck. It was a glowing white necklace.

"Wha, is this, oh no, no, no this can't be…"

"It is the necklace of the first Mistress. Yes."

Messy started bawling, unable to stop the tears.

"But, but, no, no it was lost. It was lost. How…"

"All that is lost may once more be found, my Queen. It took a great many years and a lot of favors but I found it. I found it and it's finally where it belongs."

"Oh Vix how, how can I…"

"You have given me more than I could ever have asked or hoped for, my Queen. You have given me your heart - the rarest and most beautiful of all things."

And for a few moments, a brief few moments all there was was love and happiness.

The eye of the storm.

X

Had the setting sun not been so bright during the afternoon perhaps Messy would have seen the smoke she was looking for because the rumors that had been swirling was true – the Black Machines were being revived. Deep in the hills the rocks had been removed and the Black Machines had been pulled out of their hiding places and had been started again and as they awoke, one by one, digging their teeth into the dirt and grass and their infernal engines roared to life with white fire that would scorch the ground and burn the sky and inch by inch would swallow the Kingdom of Man whole until nothing was left.

When the people would come together and talk none could quite remember what had begun the initial aggression against the Kingdom of Man or who had been the ones to start the war machines again but one thing they agreed on was that it had all begun with the dreams. The dreams were of fire and screaming and the marching of soldiers into their nation as well as Pandas and other creatures, all lead by Queen Messy and nothing to stop them. All fell before the massive army as they laid waste to everything before them. There was no hope. There was only darkness. From that darkness though there came a calm voice that was like cool water, a voice that became a bright light that forced back the darkness and pushed back the armies. The Queen hissed and she howled in rage as she chased after her soldiers. The voice had saved them. It was a woman's voice who told them she was a protector of the lands, a woman who had dealt with the witch that ruled the Kingdom of Man before and she was here now, in their dreams to remind them that the Mistresses of Magic lived to rule and that this evil Queen would someday try to take over all the lands to unite them under their red flag. The day of her attack was coming. She would conquer the lands and then release the monsters of the Thicket to rule the world.

The Thicket.

How they hated it. The Thicket's shadow had grown long across the lands and the talk of the evil things within it had spread far and wide. The place and everything within it and everything that had come from it was evil and it all needed to be burned to the ground.

The dreams came every day for weeks on end until almost everyone in the nation could hear the voice of the woman from the dream speaking to them while they were awake. First stop the witch. Then burn the Thicket. Someone was coming. Someone was coming to lead them against the witch and her people and when that day came the sky would burn and the enemies would be revealed and turned to dust and the shadow of the Thicket would be no more.

And so it was that no one quite knew who re-opened the caves and freed the Black Machines that had been penned up and put away since Queen Mey had averted the last war so many years before. Walled up and forgotten the beasts were but not dead, no, just sleeping. Waiting. Forgotten by most for generations and become but myths and stories but someone knew they still existed, someone hadn't forgotten them and this person came to the people in dreams and lead them back to the Black Machines and showed them how to awaken them once more. The Black Machines, ah but to call them machines though was not telling the full truth as these great, hulking things that were made of flesh and bone and metal and stone and which scorched sky and air and devoured all they came into contact with. Machines that screamed and howled and were things of tempered rage just barely controlled by their masters. And what did it take to wake the beasts? It took magic, blood magic, old magic, dark magic, and the like that had not been performed since the Lady Hush walked the lands. Of the great group of people that went to wake the machines a few were chosen as the blood and a young boy came forward to speak the words as others did the work of setting the machines free. The Black Machines roared to life and with that roar everyone suddenly awoke and screamed to see what they had done. Some ran to find a way to stop the machines, to turn them off but it was too late. It was too late. The voice was no longer whispering to them but was commanding them, forcing them with an unseen will that dragged through their minds and showed them a world of fire and soot.

Obey me or this will be your world. Obey me or this will be your home. Obey me or fall before me.

And the people, realizing too late what they had done marched out of the caves and tunnels and back home to await the one that would lead them. The one that would tell them what came next. And it was the blood, blood spilled that had bonded them one and all to their new master, a sin that opened a link that would not easily be broken. A red magic that now drove them to war.

War.

In the darkness between worlds where the vilest of things dwell, a place of neither life nor death a thing laughed and laughed and laughed. The Queen and her Kingdom had no hope. With Hush's Daughter and Son awakened and the other Kingdoms falling in line there would be nothing to stop the end of all things and the reign of an Inferno King. It was perfect and what better day to begin the machines of destruction and to start a war than on All Hearts Day, the one day when it was said that arms would be laid down and friendship should take over the heart. The one day when the flames of war were to be extinguished in favor of laughter, dancing, singing, and joy.

What better day to start a war?

Water always tasted sweeter with a little blood in it.

X

The eye of the storm.

The unblinking eye that sees all, the good, the evil, and the vast landscape in between.

The eye of the storm.

The animals could sense the change in the air. The earth could feel the vibrations of the machines. Even the people of the Kingdoms near and far woke in cold sweats from dark dreams of a woman that was as much tree as she was woman, sitting on a throne of fire and wearing a crown made of bones and to either side of her were two things, one covered in fire and other covered in darkness, the two of them hunched forward like hounds waiting to be released. In the dream the witch on the throne would smile wickedly and raise a large black scepter with a flame on the end and when she began to lower the scepter the dreamer would awaken, covered in sweat and shaking from fear.

Something was coming.

Darkness.

But there was yet light.

In the trees the Bumble Kitties purred their songs.

Along the riverbanks the Giraffes tended to their newborns.

In the flatlands the bugs buzzed and the Thunderlops chased one another through the high grass.

And even as a long shadow began to spread over the land young people, heads full of the warm winds of the day and giddy with the All Hearts Day Celebrations stole kisses as the sun went down. Some were rewarded with a quick hand to their face, others with a kiss in return and some got a shy smile and a grabbed and held hand and the distant sound of a door into the future being opened.

The eye of the storm.

The black eyes of rising tyrants.

Even in the blackest night there is the spark of light waiting but to be freed.

X

The nightmares and rumors spread like weeds to the lands that surrounded the Kingdom of Man and one by one the Black Machines roared to life and the Old Magic, the fire magic, the blood magic, was brought back into the world. The whispers of the Son were an infection that played on old fears and hatred of the Thicket and for a Kingdom and people many didn't trust or understand and envied. The Queen had not been to the other Kingdoms in years and this became a matter of too much time for her and her advisors to plan a new war with their Panda allies. Yes. The voice in the dreams told them this and more. War. That was what the witch was plotting. War. Better to strike first than to wait until the enemy was burning everything you loved to the dirt and you were left standing in the ash. And did they not believe that the witch had a plan for the Thicket, a diabolical plan to loose the monsters within it on the rest of the world? Of course she did, the voice in the dreams whispered, why else would she protect it as she did if she didn't. Yes, yes, the Kingdom of Man must be stopped.

The Son remained in the shadows, awakened from the mud where he had fallen and buried himself and where he had lain for decades. By the time his mother had awakened him his body was as much a part of the earth as his eyes and arms were a part of the fire that he held in his heart. He had been happy in the darkness. He had been at peace and the fire in him had subsided. Then his mother's voice came to him as a red light out of the darkness, penetrating and insistent and refusing to let him alone. *Rise. Rise. RISE!* And so he had. He awakened to intense pain and remembered the attack that had taken his men and had burned and scarred his body. He rose out of the muck and screamed from the pain and slowly pulled himself from the dirt, tearing the roots from his body and washing himself clean in the nearby river, his body. He looked at his reflection and saw how badly he was scarred terribly but as he looked into the water he saw his body begin to glow dimly then as he watched it became brighter and brighter and brighter until he wore a robe of fire and a crown of ash and he recalled what his mother called him as a boy, her red prince and his sister, yes, sister, he had had a sister, what did mother call her...she called her the black princess. Yes. He smiled and recalled those days so long ago when mother taught them about the world, about their power, and about the Thicket. He smiled and stretched his arms out wide. Yes, he would be her red prince and he would make this land pay for what they had done to her as he slept. They would pay. The Son closed his eyes and he could feel his mother's hand on his cheek, could hear her telling him how much she loved him, and could smell the dirt and earth on her as she buried her children away in the ground before a Panda attack. And that had been his childhood – hiding, fearing, hating, and then fighting. His mother had told them she was a queen once, of a place within the

Thicket but that she had dared to venture into the world outside of that place and was now nothing as she scrambled to find food and shelter for her children every night. They grew up fast. They had to. She wove spells on her children to make their bodies and minds stronger and to age them quickly so they could fight alongside her. There was a war being waged against them and they must fight.

It was time he took the war to them.

He wasn't sure where his Sister was. He felt her but they had never been close. Their mother hadn't let them be. But they could sense one another he sensed her. Alive. Awake. Angry.

The Son turned his attention to the world around himself. He was in thick woodland but he could reach his mind out and feel the presence of men and women – a village. These people worked the land and harvested the trees. They would be the first to join him. The first. Before that could happen though he must prepare for them and show them that he was a prince and that it was his Will they would follow. He turned his attention to the land around him and smiled as he found a large hollow stump and he sent his fire to scorch it and when he had done that he made several large nearby boulders lift and place themselves around the stump and to finish it he burned the tress around the makeshift throne and he was happy. He sat upon his throne and turned his mind back to the nearby village and he reached into people's minds, into their dreams and directed them that he had arrived, their prince had arrived and one by one his army came to him, first the animals, then the children, then the adults and slowly his army drew together. This was but one land but it was enough because in this land there were the Black Machines. Far away from this place in another land his mother was already raising another army, this one just as dangerous and just as terrifying. And none would defy them. None. Because no one would defy Mother. All she had to do was to say *Hush* and any thoughts of dissent would quickly fade. The Son smiled as the first of the animals in his army appeared and knelt before him.

X

As the Son and Lady Hush worked on the populace above the Daughter worked on the things below. Within the void the Daughter had found other things that were trapped there as well, things from times and eras now dim, creatures that were sent here as punishment and because there was no other place for them to go. Things that were weaker than she was and which were easily lead. Things that hungered revenge and to live within the world outside of the vast nothingness. They would do whatever it took to be free of the void. The Daughter gathered these things around her and told them of the land above, of the sun, of the warmth, and reminded them what it was like to be free. Ah, but there was something standing in there way – the humans, the Pandas, the Giraffes, all of the world above hated them and would never let them free of the darkness. They would have to take what they wanted and punish all who stood against them. The things of the void agreed, desperate to be free again and together they began to tear at the Void and to push at it and slowly, slowly a hole began to appear and as the sunlight of the world of Life poured in more things drew to the hole and began tearing and chewing and stabbing at it and slowly it became bigger and bigger and bigger and...

X

The noise in the Thicket was starting to get to Ashley. He had lived here for a great many years and had never heard it this wild – the trees crashing together, the animals howling, and the ground itself rumbling. He had come to realize long ago that the Thicket always knew what was happening in the Lands of Man long before anything or anyone else did and it would react to it accordingly. When it was calm in the world things were calm in the Thicket. When the world was in turmoil there was trouble. He had never seen it this wild though. Never. He had also never heard of it ever being this upset or read it in any of the records that No One had given him. Things had gotten so bad that even the Bumble Kitties, his constant companions on the lonely hill all this time had gone down the large hill and had settled in the distant trees. Ashley was trying to focus, to concentrate and meditate using the Sighing Pipe to clear his thoughts so he could look far off to the distance, where the clouds were growing thick to see what was happening but the sounds behind and around him roused him from his thoughts. A Seeing Stone only SHOWED the world, it didn't give a FEEL for the world like a Sighing Pipe did. He took a deep breath and closed his eyes and blew on the Sighing Pipe and hummed to himself and slowly, slowly all thoughts drifted away and his mind filled with thick, gray smoke and with it came the red clouds of hatred. Far in the distance there was movement, there was a shape, there was a figure. Ash gritted his teeth and concentrated as hard as he could and for a moment, an instant he saw a horribly burned person sitting on a throne holding a scepter with a Meep Sheep skull atop it and around the person was an army of people who knelt before them and around all of them was fire so much fire.

An inferno.

And there was so much hate.

So much anger.

Ash fell out of the vision with a start and behind him the forest shook and howled and from it came the voice of Anamare.

"What did you see?"

"You know what I saw. You *know* what I saw. All of you know. You know and do nothing to stop it."

"It is not ours to stop…even if we could. Our magic is different now. We are different. There is nothing we can do to stop this."

"So you'll leave it to your daughter? To your

granddaughters? To the people and creatures of this land that will die for this war?"

There was a long pause and then an answer.

"Yes. Yes, because we have no choice. There are some powers that even we cannot stand against. We have done what we could; there is nothing more we can do."

Ashley clenched his teeth and fists with rage and rose from the stump he used as a seat and headed into his shack to find the Summon Stone. He needed a Panda, and fast.

He had to see the Queen.

If the Mistresses wouldn't intervene he would.

If this war wasn't stopped soon it might not be stopped at all.

Aribel was just climbing out her bedroom window when she felt a sharp pain in her left leg. She looked down into the darkness and saw something bright emerge from the nothingness just in time to see it glance off her arm. She cursed and dropped out of the window and fell through the warm night air and just before she was going to hit the cobble stones she tilted her head down and blew a puff of air out and slowed her descent and landed on her bare feet without harm, spinning around quickly to see who had been throwing things at her. She wasn't surprised in the least to see Beliar sitting with her legs crossed on the stones playing with small orbs of light.

"Nice shot, ya jerk. How long have you been down here, Beli?" Aribel asked, annoyed.

"Fifteen minutes, maybe a little less."

"So where are the guards? I was expecting to have to use one of the Shadow Stones to sneak by."

"Ah, well, from my window I put the thought in their minds that they really needed to use the bathroom and it couldn't wait and away they went. The bigger question is how five large guards will manage to use a one person bathroom but that sort of math never made sense to me." Beliar looked up at her sister for the first time and smiled from behind the hair in her face.

"You're ridiculous. I don't even understand how you can do things like that but I sorta love it, ya jerk. So why are you down here?"

"I knew you were coming out and figured I'd join you."

"How did...join me where? I don't even know why I am down here. I was dozing off and woke up when I was climbing out of the window and you hit me with your *whatever* it was you threw at me. So I am going somewhere?"

"I dunno Ari, that's up to you. I just caught a glimpse of your dream and woke up and figured you could use a hand. Don't *you* know where you're going?"

"I..." As Beliar watched Aribel's eyes got distant and her shoulders slumped and she started away from the Palace and towards the edges of the royal estate.

Unsure what was going on Beli followed her sister, the feeling that she needed help stronger than ever. The girls made their way silently cross the bricked walkway that ran from white to pale yellow to yellow to light orange to orange to red and then to grass as they made their way onto the Palace lawn.

The stars were out but muted by a light haze that seemed to grow into thick clouds nearer the horizons wherever Beli looked. The hour must have been very late indeed because the two sisters were the only ones out and the lawn was alive with the sounds of bugs and the night things but as soon as the girls came near they quieted and dimmed and only began again when they had passed quietly by. The girls passed through the long rows of topiaries and the trees, ten of which had been planted at the passing of every Mistress of Magic. Far off Beli could see the courtyard where the statues of the Mistresses stood and the pieces of sculpture their mother had done. Beli paused a moment as she realized that among the familiar statues and sculptures there was something new – a gleaming white stone nearly ten feet tall and tools all around it. They were getting ready to start carving the statue of their mother. Since the first statue was place all of them were created in the Garden of Queens as it was called and it was always understood that when the work was done the Queen would step down and her reign would end. Beli felt a heavy weight in her chest but had no time to dwell on it as Aribel was some ways ahead of her and walking over towards the courtyard and as she did Beliar quickly followed, her eyes watching for sentries, guards, or worse yet Pandas. They were lucky to have snuck out with so many guards protecting them and to tempt fate this way was asking a lot but Aribel walked as if in a trance and Beliar knew there was no stopping her. Not until she'd reached where she was going.

Aribel reached the Garden of Queens and passed through the open gates and ran her hand across the statues as she passed them, her fingers lighting up as they touched the marble. She walked dazed between the large art pieces her mother had made and stopped at large piece of marble where her mother's statue would be built. Beliar jogged the last of the way to her sister, her nightgown catching in a breeze and dancing above her feet as she caught up to Aribel, who was standing now, transfixed by something at her feet. When she got to Ari she looked down at what she was looking at – there was a sketch of what the statue was to look like and words that were to be engraved on it. There was a picture of the Queen as a girl, smiling and with her arms wide and a Meep Sheep at her feet and beside it was the story of how she became a Mistress of Magic, told sparingly and leaving out much of the shading that makes a story a life. All of this it appeared would be part of a separate plaque that would sit beside the statue, as had been done with the others. The girls knew the story of their mother's rise very well, though their mother hadn't told them much. What they knew they had been told by their father, Gloof, Arnk, and had even seen it in their history lessons. They mother would never tell them much though. She didn't like to talk about herself, only about the Kingdom, and her own mother, Queen Anamare, and the arts, and the world, and the girls, but never herself. She even went so far as to tell the girls – we'll talk about this some other day – when they would ask about the stories they'd heard. The story of their mother stopped at the marriage to their father but it was clear by the space that was left that there was much more that had yet to be put down. Beli looked from the parchment that lay on the stones to the marble and she felt tears welling up. Suddenly Ari took her hand. She was back again.

"When do you think it will happen, Beli?"

"I dunno, Ari, soon I guess. We're just about the age when she made the choice and Grandmother Anamare went away. Our mother's Queen for a lot longer than most of the others. Her time is coming to a close and judging by what's here someone expects it to be pretty soon."

"Where will she go, Beli? Into the trees like the others? Will dad go with her?"

"He can't go into the trees with her. No men ever go. At least, that's what the books say. They always die or just disappear from history but it seems like they don't go into the woods though I am not sure that's true. I have read some older histories that talk about some of the Kings being there as well, but who can really say?"

"What do you think is back in there, Beli? Is it…is it death?"

"Yes. And no. It's just...not here. It's somewhere else. I don't know where. To read the stories it sounds as if all of the Queens simply become Mistresses of Magic and oversee the lands, watching over things. I don't know if I believe that because a lot of bad stuff has happened and they never stopped it but then, maybe that's not for them to do. Maybe they just...whisper to us...in our dreams. Making sure we know everything will be OK in the end."

"Oh..." Aribel trailed off and ran her hands along the smooth marble where the statue would emerge from before turning to look off into the distance.

"Do you know where the Kings are buried, Beli?"

"I think it's on the other side of the Palace, in a..."

"No, the *Old* Kings."

Beliar's stomach rolled. She knew. She had been a little girl running wild and crazy and had found where the Old Kings rested but before she could enter the area Arnk had grabbed her roughly and had told her she was never, ever, *ever* to go in there. It was sacred ground. Haunted ground. Forbidden ground. She was very defiant as a child but she never defied Arnk this one demand and had broken down into tears after his stern lecture and he had lifted her and carried her most of the way back, letting her walk the rest of the way home when she had stopped crying. Yes, she knew where it was. The Old Kings rested at the edge of the Kingdom of Man. On the way back Arnk had told her that secretly the resting place of the Old Kings was full of old magic, bad magic, red magic and that many people had disappeared from that area never to be seen again. It had been a place that the Lady Hush had performed many black rituals to mock the Queens. It was said, he told her, that something of the old witch still remained there, even in her absence, waiting for someone to bring her back to our world. It scared Beli then and scared her now but that fear was nothing to what she felt as she looked at her sister and watched in stunned silence as Aribel's face twisted into a nasty smile.

"*I* know where they are. I have been there. The woman in my dream showed me where it was. She says mother doesn't want us to go there but that it's our birth right as future Queens. It's beautiful there. She's shown me things. Magic. Forbidden magic. I can show you. I can show you everything. Come on, I'll show you." Aribel walked past her sister and began heading towards the hill and Umwood beyond.

"I don't think that's a good idea, Ari, let's, let's just go back inside. We can get something to eat and talk about that boy I have seen you talking to down in the village. What's his name? Is it...Matthew?" Beli forced a smile, hoping her sister would wake from her trance at this.

"Oh, so you're scared, like usual? You're predictable. I thought you were supposed to be the *wild* one. The one who liked to sneak out with the boys from the Carnival when it was in town. The one who liked *dark* things and had *done* dark magic. You're like Mother. Afraid. Afraid of everything you don't understand. A coward." Beliar couldn't see her sister's face but knew there was an awful grin there, a grin that wasn't hers. Beliar's hands itched and in the distance she thought she heard the sound of a Kreep Sheep, which were always near when she was upset. Hidden from sight so others wouldn't see them but there for her just the same. She suddenly noticed her eyes were burning along with her cheeks and she felt a rising tide of anger in her. Anger at the other, the one inside of her sister, not at Aribel.

"Shut up."

"Come, come. Did you think no one knew? Knew of those boys you kissed in the dark near the lake? Or the trips into Umwood you take every month to see your pet Kreep Sheeps, oh, and to check and make sure that the Daughter hasn't pulled herself out of the dark place you put her? Oh, I know a lot about what you do, little sister. A *whole* lot. But don't worry, I would never hurt you, no...the Daughter will do that for me."

Little sister was something Aribel only called her when she was being nasty, and even then it was a joke. They were twins, born only a minute apart but it was still something one sister could say to the other out of spite. This though, this was different. This wasn't Aribel saying this. It wasn't Aribel at all. Beliar felt fire in her hands, black fire, but gritted her teeth against the push to use it. Instead she looked to the sky and saw one dark cloud, then another spin down from the sky and land on either side of her, issuing their customary greeting as they appeared.

"Kreeeeeep."

Beliar smiled when her sister hissed at the arrival of the Kreep Sheeps.

"Oh goody, your pets are here. They'll make

wonderful coats for my children." Aribel hiss again.

Beliar went down to her knees and petted the Kreep Sheeps, a hand for each, and leaned close to them and whispered a word which they responded to with grunts of understanding and then they began to waddle towards Aribel, who took a step away from them. Undaunted the Kreep Sheeps kept approaching and she kicked a foot out at them and caught one in the head and stopped it. It huffed loudly and shook its head and made two fluttering hops and took up a position beside Ari, opposite the other Sheep. Beliar smiled. Aribel took a step away and the Sheeps moved with her, another step and they did the same. She did this for several steps and when they kept moving with her she stopped and lowered herself and reached down and grabbed them roughly by the horns and lifted them up and as soon as they were in hand there was a scent of something burning. Beliar rushed forward but before she got to her sister Aribel had thrown the Sheep away, one to the East and the other to the West, both of them letting out howls of pain as they were thrown. Beliar was on her in a step and had her sister's face in her hands and as she grabbed Ari the veil that had slipped over the moon lifted and she saw not her sister but a withered old woman's face, grinning with a toothless mouth. Beliar's mind turned to fire and she pulled her sister close and kissed her forehead and as she did she passed the fire from her mouth and through Aribel and Ari shuddered and tried to pull away but Beli held her close, her hands holding her sister tight to her until at last a long cold breath poured from her mouth and after that Beli finally released her sister.

"You do not belong here, monster. Be gone. Back to the grave. Back to the abyss."

"Ah, little girl, look to the horizon and witness your mother's legacy and your inheritance. You shall inherit fire and ash and nothing more and before this war is over you will meet my daughter again, my dear, and you won't like what she brings with her. You won't like it at...all."

The old woman smiled then Ari's face went slack and Aribel was back again, back and dazed.

"Beli, Beli where, where..." Aribel's face went white and she bent to the side and retched and Beliar held her as she lost her balance. Beliar looked to the horizon where the long tendrils of smoke came from and for the first time she noticed a scent in the air she hadn't smelled before – the scent of fire.

X

"And had I not found you girls we would all..."

"Gloof..."

"...in more trouble than you can..."

"Gloof...."

"...imagine. I have seen your mother not just angry but *very angry* and it is nothing you would ever care to..."

"*GLOOF!*"

"What Beliar, what? And quiet now, you'll wake..."

"It's come Gloof. It's come."

"What has come, girl? What has come?"

"The war…"

X

There was a thin mist along the ground where the Old Kings had lain silent for hundreds of years nothing stirred. The land was overgrown with weeds and exposed roots and the statues that had been placed here were covered in thick ivy. The trees of Umwood swayed back and forth under the spell of a heavy wind but stopped suddenly. The wind stopped and all was still a moment before the ground erupted in the center of the statues and a fissure opened wide. Cracks

spread out from the center and three of the
newest and smallest statues tipped inward
and fell into the hole and disappeared. The
ground buckled upwards again and more dirt
fell in. The earth shifted and the oldest
statue, a stone carving of the head of the first
of the Old Kings cracked and the front of the
face crumbled into the weeds. Slowly, quietly
arms, tentacles, claws, and feelers rose out of
the hole and one by one the things of the
Void came into the world of Man once more.
The things filled the field and spilled into the
forest, a quiet but restless army waiting to be
lead. The last of the things to emerge was the
Daughter who pulled itself from the void and
inhaled deeply the world it had been torn
from by the young witch, the daughter of the
Queen. The Daughter rose to its full height
and clattered its teeth together and the rest of
its tribe did the same. It extended its long,
wood arms and embraced two of the tall
Kings and pulled them down almost gently,

as if it was no effort and taking the cue of their leader the rest of the army tore away at the statues, ripped trees from their roots, and ate deep of the earth, devouring the grass, the stone, the weeds, and dirt and moving slowly Westward as they did, a slow plague that would eat everything in their path until they reached the Palace, the Queen, and the young witches. The Daughter smiled to imagine how sweet those little morsels would taste as they screamed their way down its throat and she slowly began moving West.

X

The Great Loneliness looked out over its domain and was pleased. All around its trunk was a thick black lake that bubbled with life. Inch by inch it was rotting the Thicket, its roots sucking the life from the land and tree by tree came under its control was uprooted and repositioned to create a perimeter around the Great Loneliness so no enemies could get close to harm it as it raised its army. At every move and attack on the Thicket there was no reprisal and the Loneliness was shocked at this. There had always, *always* been a counter to any aggressions in the past but something was going on. Something was distracting the Thicket from this threat deep in its heart. The Great Loneliness wasn't powerful enough to know what was happening outside of the Thicket yet and it needed to know what was happening. It needed to know what was so great and deadly that the Thicket was unaware of what happened at its heart. It needed an emissary It needed...

The Panda.

The Panda had turned on its kind and pledged its support but had disappeared not long after it had first introduced itself to the Great Loneliness and now it had returned after days of being away.

And it wasn't alone.

The Panda returned from the wilds of the Thicket with four more of its kind, three of them identical with their black and white and large frames and the last of them was a War Panda, beasts known as fearless and dangerous when angered but fiercely loyal to their kind. This was interesting indeed.

"I come with word of what is happening beyond the Thicket and with word of what comes next and I have brought with me...similarly minded friends who wish to see what you have planned." Zum said with a smile.

"Ah, you are a crafty boy, aren't you? I happily welcome you and your friends. So, tell me, what is happening now...And what comes next?"

"First, a bit of a re-introduction, so we are all on the same page - I am Zum of the Panda tribe, Zum the Protected, Zum the Favored, Zum the Second. You have not heard of me but I have heard of you, Oh Great Loneliness. We *all* have heard of you. We are the Thicket Tribe who was abandoned by our clan when they fled into the Land of Man. When they left we were told to protect the Home Tree and to watch over the forests. We were forced to fend for ourselves. My father was Jerf the Betrayer and after his attempt to slay the mate of the Panda's Umph he was exiled to the Outer World where he died, killed within days of his exile by the beasts of Hush, your daughter. My father left behind my mother, three sisters, and me. Once my father was gone and Loof and the others left the Thicket the attention of the tribe was turned back to my family and we were sent to come live here, near you and away from the safety of the rest of the tribe and so it was here, in your shadow where I grew up. Where my mother died, poisoned by your black lakes. Here where my sisters were devoured as cubs by the things you had spawned. Here, where I grew to hate the rest of my tribe and where I escaped from as a Mid-Cub and where I now return. Hello, enemy, I am Zum, and I am here to serve you."

This was a lot for the Great Loneliness to take in. Its mind reeled. Time was a stone in deep water that it could not retrieve. It had been so long since it had been conscious, since it had been part of this world and yet all the things Zum said seemed familiar, like dreams or memories that were fading to gray. In the heart of all of this chaos was one thought – enemy. The Great Loneliness sent its poisoned roots closer to the Pandas and bent its body close to them as a friend, and co-conspirator.

"Goodness. I had no idea. I have been asleep for so many years I cannot say I recall any of this. I am deeply sorry for any ills I have caused your…"

"No lies, monster. There is no reason to lie to us, Enemy. No reason. We know what you are. You are the evil that came from above to plague this land and to spread the seeds of your hatred. You birthed the greatest evil that has ever come to this land and are a Cancer. There is no need to shy from it. We know what you are. We know…and we welcome it."

Curious. Very curious. The Great Loneliness leaned closer, its branches untangling from the ones around it, no longer trying to be a friend but now something more. Something much more.

"So why then, after all the horrible things you lay before me, why come to me if not to declare war? Why do you come into the spider's web when you know I am venomous and happy to strike? Why do you court death when I am happy to oblige you?"

The Great Loneliness pulled its trees in around the Pandas in a tight circle and readied its roots to strike. One kiss from their barbs and there would be no more Zum, nor his companions.

"We come because that was the past and I care not for the past. None of us do. We are outcasts. Left by our tribe to die in the Thicket and banished to live in your shadow. We have waited for this moment, for the dawning of the precipice, for the edge of the war for you to awaken. We are here to join you against the Thicket and against the rest of this horrible world. We offer you a truce, monster, and shall do your bidding until the day this world is on fire and then on that day we shall deal with you. That is what we offer." Zum said, indifferent to the trees that had positioned themselves close to him and his companions.

"You mention war. What war?" Asked the Loneliness, pulling away from the Pandas and rising again, stretching as the black lake bubbled with rage.

"Your child Hush and two of her many children, the only two she dared to love, have come home to seek revenge for her death. The Witch that leads the humans in the Kingdom of Man has made herself quite the friend to my people and seeks to finally unite the Kingdoms before the end of her reign. Her plans have been seen and overheard. She wants a lasting peace. She has labored for years on a last piece of art that will bring all together under a rainbow flag of friendship. She will not have her peace. We are here; *I* am here to tear all of this down. I want you to consume this world with rot and to take everything into the darkness where you came from. I want you destroy everything. And I want to help you. After that I make no promises of allegiance. After the world is gone you and I have much to discuss. This is what we bring. This is what we offer" Zum went down on one knee and as he did so did the others

The Great Loneliness in its wisdom and madness split the bark along its front into a false smile.

"Well, then let's begin."

X

It was three days since All Hearts Day but Messy was still glowing from the news that Vix was staying here. What had at first come as embarrassing news had quickly turned to relief as the uneasy feeling in her gut grew. She didn't feel connected to anyone or anything these days and had become consumed with the art she was working on. The one last piece she wanted to complete before she stepped aside and let her daughters take the throne. One last piece to unite everyone...or divide them forever. She knew something was wrong with her daughters but every time she tried to speak to them nothing came out because there was too much to say and too much that needed to be said. It was a flood that she knew she must contain or drown in so she had built a wall around herself and her heart to protect the ones she loved. That wall was collapsing.

Something was going on but she was too clouded to see it. Even the Seeing Stone would not come clear to show her the Kingdoms. If she was cloudy, it was cloudy and right now she could barely think straight. It was funny; all of this had started when she had tried to help the Kingdom find their way out of from under the gray, overcast skies, when she had tried to help them find some happiness once more yet here she was living under those same black clouds every day. The Meep Sheep had grown in number over the many years and some days they would fill the sky with their own cloud formations but there was always one near to the Queen, the first Sheep, always by her side. Her constant companion. Her never wavering friend. Messy wondered sometimes if the Sheep's fate was tied to her own, if, when she finally entered the Mother Wood, it would follow behind her and disappear as she did.

She shuddered and tears came to her eyes.

War. Death. The Mother Wood. More gray thoughts on an otherwise beautiful day. A day that, oddly, featured snow. Messy looked out her window and saw no clouds – it was a clear blue day with a warm breeze. She held her hand out and caught a few flakes and they were gray on her pale flesh. She ran her thumb over the snow and it smeared black against her skin and her heart began racing as soon as she realized that it wasn't snow at all but ash. It was snowing ash. Messy looked off to the horizon and saw that the clouds there were getting darker and thicker. She didn't need to hear the rumors of war that were spreading to know that within a day or two the rumors would spread like a plague of words and the Kingdom would be in a panic.

The people should be panicked.

    The struggles with the neighboring Kingdoms were an ever present threat but there had not been full out war for many, many years. Something was different though. Something was pushing this and fanning flames that had been smoldering to nothing. Whatever this new threat was, new or old, it was the worst threat in a very long time, since the time when the hills and valleys had run red, and this threat was coming from all sides. Messy had disbanded the army years earlier as a sign that her people had no interest in war but at the urging of her advisors there was a bell that was to be wrung three times and if it was wrung it meant that war was coming and that all able bodied people needed to get their families to safety and to arm themselves.

Messy looked up and far above the terrace where she stood was the bell, a bright silver that shimmered as the light hit it, silent and waiting to be called to duty and Messy knew that that bell would ring, and soon.

Messy turned her attention away from the bell, and the horizon, and the war and went back into her studio, shutting the door to the terrace as she did and almost locking her Meep Sheep out. She bent down and patted her old friend on the head then went back to her stool and sat heavily upon it and returned to her work while outside the first news of the coming war was starting to spread.

X

When Ashley arrived in the Queen's Citadel he headed straight for Messy, Skraw, and the She-Panda who had brought him happy to wait for the human outside in the sun. As Ash quickly made his way up the pathway towards the Palace he smiled to see his old friend Vix ahead of him but that smile quickly fell when his way was barred by first the guards and then by the King himself, who put an arm around Ash and lead him away from the entrance to the Palace. Ash became frantic as he tried to talk to the King, to explain to him what was happening and how dire the situation was but he only got a pat on the shoulder and a sad smile.

"We know."

"You *what*?" Ash asked, shaking from anger.

"We know. Now please, take some rest in the

guest cottage and Messy will see you as soon as she's able. You have my word."

Ash was told that the Queen would love to see him but that she was in the middle of a project that had her full attention and that, if he would but wait for her, he would indeed be able to see her. But not right away. Ash opened his mouth and again the King shook his head.

"We know." Having said this a third time the King patted Ashley's shoulder one last time and then turned and walked away and back inside, leaving Ash to stare after him silently. Frustrated, Ash went to walk after the King but a heavy paw fell on his shoulder, stopping him.

"Let him go." Said Skraw.

"But..."

"He knows. At least some of what you came

to say. He knows. It's written on his face." Skraw was staring after the form of the King as he disappeared.

"Then this is a waste of time. A complete waste..." Ash turned away from the Palace but the familiar paw held him from leaving.

"No. It's not. They don't know everything. And neither do you."

"What do you mean? I know about the war..."

"You know about the boy, the one on the throne, the one bathed in fire, you know about him. You don't know about the Thicket though. You don't know what is happening and honestly, you don't know what scares me, what scares all of us. Even The Great Loof, who is at the twilight of his long reign, doesn't know the full story of what is happening. There is a change in the land, we can sense that, can smell it, just as we smell the ash of the Black Machines, but there is more at work. More than just the bloodlust of Man."

"What else is there? It's Hush, clearly it's Lady Hush behind this but what else could there be?"

"There is more than just the witch, Ashley of Pickles. Much more. We just don't know how much more."

"Well, are you looking into it?" Ash and Skraw made their way to the edge of the wide stone space that lead up to the Palace and stood near the ornate pink wall and lowered their voices.

"We have sent out four parties, one in each direction, North, South, East, and West, to get a better feel for what was happening in the Kingdom and none have returned. None.

Each took with them a War Panda and a collection of enchanted stones to protect themselves but it has been weeks since they left and we have no idea what happened. None."

"This is…this…and with the Thicket so upset…" Ash had his hands clenched before him and was looking at his boots. There were so many things filling his mind. Dangerous, terrible things.

"The Thicket knows something is wrong. Many of us come from there, from its seeds. It knows we are in danger. But that is not the worst, friend Ashley."

"What do you mean?"

"Ashley, I have not told anyone else this so I tell you this in confidence," Skraw was standing on her hind legs and dropped down onto all fours to speak so just Ash heard and he marveled at the beauty of her fur, which changed color in the sunlight.

"I am the daughter of the son of Loof, you know my father as Gloof, and I am trusted, like all my family is, as protectors to the crown and that was why I came for you this day. I am not an escort but this day I made an exception. I needed to speak to you. I am a sentry and I work the outer edge of the Panda Kingdom and I have found circling our lands, small skulls on stakes placed a few feet apart. They appeared literally overnight."

"When did you find them Skraw?"

"Two nights ago. And when I removed them I told no one but this morning I found more. They were Panda skulls, Meep Sheep skulls, Bumble Kitty Skulls, and there were human skulls as well. This is more than war, Ashley, this is something much darker than just that and none of us is prepared."

"Then what is it?"

"This smells like revenge."

Ash was silent after this and remained that way as Skraw ushered him into the guest home that stood at the edge of the property. Inside the home was a chef and a servant and they were ready for their guests. Skraw and Ash were given meals and were asked if there was anything else and when the servant and cook were told that they were no longer needed they took their leave. Ash was lost in his thoughts so he barely noticed when Skraw left him to meet with her father near the river that ran through the citadel. Ash wanted more than anything to leave, to be back at the Thicket and to prepare to defend it but he knew that he had to make sure the Queen understood what was happening. He hadn't seen her in ages and from what he had been told she had withdrawn and was obsessed with some art piece she was working on that was keeping her from many of her usual duties. Even now, as the machines of war are marching for her Kingdom how could she ignore it and just keep...doodling? He had never understood her art or how it came to her and had had to remind himself that he too created art just of a different kind and that when he was taken by inspiration the world seemed to fall away. Just the same though this was different. This was different. As much as he questioned her though deep down he still trusted her, and that was the thing that kept him from just leaving. He had to know how she was, and what was going on as much as he needed to tell her what he knew.

Ashley's dreams were troubled that night and filled with horrors. The only nightmare he could remember when he woke was of the Thicket in flames and he standing with a torch held high over his head, commanded by the person in the throne of fire – commanded to destroy the Thicket and then the Queen. Dream Ash turned and faced Ashley and it was a monster, its face sunken, its eyes gone, and an undead thing that wore a terrible grin. Suddenly the scene shifted and he was in the body of the thing and looking into the face of the Queen, who was on her knees and bleeding, her hands held up to ward off an attack, with her Kingdom ablaze all around her. Ash woke then and didn't sleep for the rest of the night, the nightmare's hold on him too strong to escape so instead he dressed and went and sat in the chair outside the small guest house and watched the Palace, waiting for dawn.

At some point in the early morning Ash had fallen asleep in the chair, the weight of his exhaustion so great that he finally fell into a dreamless darkness. When he woke he thought he was in the nightmare again and let out a sharp howl as he saw Messy kneeling before him, her hair dark and her eyes sad. Ash recoiled from her touch but quickly realized that it really was her and that it was not yet dawn. She put a slender finger to her lips and he clenched his jaw and nodded. She smiled weakly and put a hand against his cheek, caressing it softly before standing.

"It has been too long, my friend, and the worries of the world are showing their claw marks on you."

"Not all of us are as blessed as you, my Queen, to radiate with beauty even late into our years."

"And it has gotten late, hasn't it? So very late. What brings you here to see me, Ashley? I am sorry to have kept you waiting so long. I am just so busy right now that it's hard to break away and I tend to lose track of time and, and everything else."

"Do you know what is happening in the Kingdoms? Do you see what is coming, my Queen?"

"Yes…"

"*Do you?*"

The Queen had been looking off to the distance, to where the smoke was at the edge of the Kingdom and for the first time Ash had ever known her she looked tired and old. Hearing his question she spun back around and brought her gaze back to him and looked at Ashley with a fierceness and anger he had never seen from her before and suddenly she was the young woman he had first met, though filled with fire.

"*I KNOW!* Trust me when I say I know. I have three choices – I can run or I can fight or I can try to work one last piece of magic. I will not run. I am no fighter. All I have left is my magic. It's the only chance I have. Maybe the only chance *we* have." And then the fire was gone and she looked tired again. Ash reached out and grabbed her hands and took them in his.

"But you're not alone. Don't you see that? Messy, Queen, you are not alone. This Kingdom would follow you into the darkness, into nothingness because they believe you, they trust you, and they love you. We all love you. This isn't your burden alone and it isn't your fight alone."

"But it is, Ash, it is. I am the Queen. I am the Mistress of Magic. I knew when I put on this crown that I bore the weight of generations of Queens, of my family, of this land and its history. Did you know that my family has not always held the crown? That there were Kings? There was a time when the line was broken, when a King took the crown and, knowing how the Kingdom had come to rely on the Queen had married a woman from the South, from the magic tribe and she was made a Mistress of Magic. And did you know that we have never been free of war as the heralds will proclaim every year on the anniversary of my crowning? There are always skirmishes at the borders, always, but worse, there was a time when a tribe from across the seas tried to invade, a time when Vix had to secretly lead the Pandas against these invaders and had to send them back into the sea? My royal gown, once white has been dyed red over the years and I am tired. I am so tired of the conflicts. Tired of the secrets held from the Kingdom, and from my own family. But this is a burden I must carry. It's mine."

Her gaze dropped and she pulled her hands from Ash and took a step away and as he did he noticed she was in her sleeping gown, covered with dirt and grass and something else, was it clay? Ash stood to see her off.

"I am sorry, Messy."

Messy turned to Ash, her eyes on him again and the anger still there, just under the surface.

Sorry for what?"

"I am sorry I wasn't there for you. That none of us have been. I am sorry for the burden you have had to bear. I am sorry. But I am done being sorry. The time for sorry has passed and whether you like it or not this is not your burden any longer and we can't sit idly by and wait. Not anymore. Goodbye, my queen."

And with that Ash turned away from the

Queen and walked off towards where his companion was resting. Ash woke Skraw and told her he was ready to return home. Ready to fight. Messy, stood shaking, her eyes full of tears, and watched one of her oldest friends walk away, and hating how very alone she'd made herself.

X

The Thicket was a maelstrom and the Motherwood which rested at the heart of the Thicket was one of the last safe havens and as such was full of Bloo Moos and other native creatures trying to escape the spreading plague that was swallowing their homes. The white trees of the Motherwood woke from their long slumber and began to sing and as they sang so too did the wild Bumble Kitties that remained in the forest and the ground began to shake and a light came from the heart of the Mother Wood and the light spread out into the forest scorching the trees and turning them white as well. And from the middle of all this came a calm voice.

"It's time."

And the Motherwood awoke.

The Black Machines

They say that the Black Machines were once people. People so sad, so lost, and so lonely that when these people all shared a dream, the same dream of the Thirteenth King calling them to the Palace they went, went with the first fire of hope in them that they'd ever felt.

Come, he said *come and find your place in this world.*

And at the Palace they were all greeted by the King himself, who was a handsome young man renowned for his deeds in Border Wars. It had been the Thirteenth King who had banished the Giraffes from the Kingdom and who had dared to welcome Warlocks from across the seas to be his advisors. The night that the strangers arrived the King threw the visitors a magnificent feast and had court performers dance and sing and play music until the guests were all falling asleep from having laughed and smiled so much. Each was ushered to their luxurious room where they immediately fell asleep, happier than any of them could ever remember being and it was as they slept that the King returned to them to whisper one more thing.

You will serve.

Those first twenty people were never seen again in the Kingdom or anywhere else nor were any of the other visitors that came to the Palace every few years when similar strangers would appear at the gates and disappear inside.

In a few years no one wanted to visit the Palace, a place many called haunted, and they were not wrong and now no one goes there, but also, no one leaves. In fact, nothing leaves the Palace anymore. Not after the Thirteenth King had his full court remove themselves. After that it was only he and his

Warlocks in the Palace and the sound of chanting and the sight of strange lights late at night. It was only when the Thorks from the islands that lay between the Kingdom of Man and the Far Seas invaded did the gates of the Palace open and the Thirteenth King emerge once more. He emerged an old man, withered and bent at but forty years of age but there was still a glimmer in his eyes that told the people this was their King and he was still dangerous. He emerged to announce to the people that he would face a new enemy that threatened the land and that he would defeat them and the people believed him. His crown may have rusted but it was still their King. The people cheered and pledged their swords and arrows but the King told they that he had a new army and from out of the Palace marched the Warlocks, looking just as they had when they first arrived, and behind them was an army of iron and metal beasts that rose twelve feet into the air and walked on two legs that moved like a man's but were covered in barbs and spikes. Their arms were long and metal and where hands may have been were curved and looked to many as shovels that dug into the ground as they walked ape-like behind the King. The chests of the things were opened and revealed a raging fire that seemed to drip down their chests from the bodies of the things from time to time, burning grass, dirt, and stone to nothing and leaving a scorch at the bottom of every hole the hands dug. The head of the beasts was a black metal box with holes punched in the front where eyes looked out, human eyes. Several people fainted to see the machines and unshakeable fear went through the crowd as the things came near. The King climbed on the shoulders of one machine that was nearly fifteen feet tall and he gave a whistle and marched his army of fifty-eight Black Machines past the Village of

Loon that surrounded the Palace and he gave the people who gathered to watch the procession a merry salute as the army headed off to the border. As the Black Machines passed some said they could hear sobs and pleading coming from within the armor but were sure it was just the sound of the engines inside the things as they went past and nothing else.

The battle with the Thorks was brief and bloody and scarred the land for years after but the King returned victorious and his Black Machines proved they were things to be feared as word spread among his people and out to the other lands of the destruction they had sown. The King gave a bow from the top of his machine as he passed through Loon once more and then disappeared with his army into what people now called the Black Palace and was neither seen nor heard from for many years and the people were glad for this. The sounds they heard from the Palace and the sight of the Warlocks, who had grown to number six, passing through the gates as the sun fell and then retreating to the woodlands as the sun rose unnerved the people and there was a secret thrill among them people when the King's death was announced by one of the Warlocks. That thrill died though when it was also announced that these strangers were given the power of the throne in absence of a King and would control the land and the Black Machines until a new heir was found.

It was not long after this that the first of the wars began.

Long, bloody wars that ravaged the Kingdom and nearly destroyed it, the Black Machines destroying everything that came before them, whatever it was. There was good that came from the war though as the Warlocks were caught outside of the Palace by the people of

Loon and a battle ensued that left three of the Warlocks dead and which forced the rest into hiding in the woods. With the Warlocks gone a brave general took his forces into the Palace and cleaned it of the magical relics and statues that the Warlocks had put in place inside. The general also had his men drag the sleeping Black Machines out and they buried the things far away from the citizens and sealed them away and cursed anyone who ever woke the beasts again. It was after that that he was elected the new King and a new era of prosperity reigned for many years and slowly the Kingdom healed.

This prosperity was not to last.

PART TWO

It was just past dawn in the small village of Irrie, the furthermost village in all of the Kingdom of Man where only a handful of people lived. This was very close to where the Old Kings rested, a place long thought haunted, and was near to many of the fields where the bloodiest battles had played out but the ground here was fertile, the river was near, and the forest served as a natural defense against the neighboring Kingdom. The ground here had been so fertile that when the Kingdom of Man began to expand one man, Henrik Buttertea, a man from across the seas who knew nothing of the ghost stories of the area and no spook story would keep him away from land with vegetation so lush and green that he so gladly accepted the offer of free land that the Queen offered and decided this would be the place he would set his roots. As soon as he had marked off his land Henrik immediately set about clearing brush and tilling the soil and planting and when all of that was done he started the long work of building a home suitable for a family. Henrik took two years to accomplish the things he had set out to do since that rainy Fall morning when he first saw the Red Valley but the moment he was done he drew himself a hot bath, combed his long, wild hair and thick beard and dressed in a suit he had never worn before and he set out for Loor, the closest village, where there was a fair woman whom he had loved since he had seen her the day he rode through town on his way to his land.

The woman's, name was Bethi and she did not laugh when Henrik, three years her junior, asked to have her hand in marriage but nor did she agree. She was a widow and was breathtakingly beautiful and had two young boys to raise. She had seen a dozen men come to see her; all of them had been looking for her hand in marriage but when they learned she had young ones the men quickly disappeared back into the brush again. She had had her heart broken by man and by life and she refused to let the same happen to her boys - the death of their father was burden enough. So Bethi smiled at Henrik and said she would love to hear what this man was offering but first he needed to meet two people, and then she called her boys. And if Henrik had been in love with her at first sight he loved the boys at first laugh. The boys came running out of a small stand of trees dressed in moss and leaves and roaring like monsters and laughing between roars as they chased one another. Henrik fell from his knee to his bottom with laughter. At first Bethi's brows became thunderheads, thinking he was laughing at her boys but when she saw how the boys immediately turned their monstrous attentions on him and he just laughed all the more she smiled, secretly, and decided that perhaps, just perhaps this was a man she might want to listen to.

A year to the day he courted her Henrik married Bethi and she and her boys moved to their new home with happy hearts. The crops there were booming and with the success of those crops and the broad and joyful personality of Henrik, who was said to have left the Carnival to come to this land, others began to move to that area also and quickly this became one of the gems of the land and a place that two of the Queens vacationed while on tour of the Kingdom. The second Queen to visit was Queen Messy, who came bringing Meep Sheep, which were not often seen in this area, and with a young man who had a voice of pure sunshine named Glen. This was many years after Henrik and his family had all passed away and many years in the past but it was still a time that was remembered and to these people, who laughed more freely than they spoke, it was another thing to be proud of, in their far away village in this very big Kingdom.

Irrie was a proud, happy village and one that had anchored the Kingdom in the dark times and had helped lead it through to the light when those times passed but as the people of the village woke to do their chores and to make their breakfasts three days after All Hearts Day they rose to ruin. The Daughter and its army had made their way slowly from the statues of the Old Kings and had devoured and destroyed everything in their path, the last of them poisoning the ground with venom that bubbled as it touched the earth so that nothing would grow there again.

The mass of things marched forth in silence, speaking through their destruction instead of through words or sounds. The Daughter stayed at the rear as its army traveled but as they neared the first village it pressed forward and lead with a rage that seemed unquenchable.

For the people of the small village there was no hope.

No escape.

There was only destruction.

Animals fled from the things, running, flying, and crawling away as fast as they could go though many were caught and were but appetizers for the marching horde. Trees were uprooted by one beast as another tore apart and then a third would eat it. All grass and growth was clawed through and dug up, eaten and vomited out. The things cut a wide swathe across the land a thousand stones wide and they created a river of death that made it impossible to cross the Valley without coming in contact with the ruin. As the army moved forward the destruction they left behind them was a scar that could be seen from the neighboring Kingdom and it was seen, though not understood, and the fear there sank ever deeper, as this must be a new weapon of the witch, meant to scare them from their own deadly course. Instead of stopping the march of that Kingdom though it only served to deepen their resolve.

As for the Daughter and her army...

Onward they marched.

Onward toward Man.

The town awoke in shadow as the beasts chewed their way forward and the screams that rang out were nothing to sound of the forest being reduced to nothingness.

The Daughter broke its silence and howled with awful delight as she saw all of the villagers and felt the hunger in her rise until she could take no more.

The town of Irrie had stood through famine, through flood, through battles, through sorrow and through happiness that had been passed on from generation to generation but it could not stand against the horrors of the Void or the rage of the Daughter and within an hour there was nothing left of it but ash.

So fell Irrie.

X

The Great Loof had been sick for many weeks and it was worrying the tribe. The Great Loof was the greatest leader the Panda tribe had ever seen and with war coming the tribe was afraid what might happen without his leadership. As the smoke in the distance started to close the sky off so that only a gray dome remained Loof called for his son, Gloof.

"It is time, my son." Said Loof.

"I knew it was coming but I had hoped, I had hoped…"

"As had I. As had we all but the council has met and we have all agreed and it is time."

The Great Loof shivered and coughed and pulled the thick blanket he was under tighter around himself.

"And those that refuse?" Gloof knew that this order, which had been understood since the Pandas and the Humans mended the wounds between them, would not be one that the entire Panda Kingdom would stand for but it was the will of the Great Loof and was the will of the council and was what must be done.

Loof closed his eyes slowly and looked away from his son.

"Then you convince them. And if they will not be convinced then you tell them they may leave. And if they refuse to leave...you exile them and you hope that it goes no further than that."

"As you wish, father." Gloof hoped it wouldn't come to that but knew in his heart that the darkness was not yet here and things would get much worse before there was a hint of the sun again.

"Son, there's one more thing. I have had much time to think, much time to reminisce, and I have come to a decision - I want you to take the Crown. It's time and..."

"No."

"What? How can you refuse the Crown, the Kingdom, or the wishes of your father?"

"Father, I refuse *because* you are my father. We are at war and I am needed on the battlefield. I am needed because we have allies that need *us* and we have not had allies in a very long time. I refuse the crown because you are not yet ready to leave this place and your people. And I refuse because it is time for our people to choose who shall lead them and should we survive the war they deserve to choose the way ahead. They will have earned at least that much." Loof was embarrassed by how much he had said but it felt good to get out things he had had on his heart for some time.

"And these things, these things have been heavy upon your heart and mind these past weeks?"

"Yes father, they have."

"Ah, such a wise son I have, you shame me for my rash thoughts…"

"But…"

"Ah, but son, shame is not a bad thing when it reminds you of the wisdom of others. I have been sick a very long time and perhaps, perhaps it's time I will myself well, at least a little. Bring me the Bloo Moo juice there, on the top shelf in the black bottle. You have a hard road ahead of you and I shall stand with you, my son, and after that we shall stand aside…and let our people choose the path ahead."

"Such a wise father I have." Gloof leaned forward and Loof did the same and their foreheads touched and they nugged and wished this happy moment could last forever.

X

The hillside and forest was full of the sound of coughing and the air was thick with soot the Son though was all but indifferent to it. In the dark of the woods the Son sat on his tree stump throne, held his scepter made out of a scorched branch and small skull, and wore his crown made of vines and dead bugs and had his robes of fire wrapped around him but he felt like no King. He felt like a performer, a child acting at being daddy for the day. He felt like a fraud. The Son rose from his throne and looked out to the Kingdom below. He was at the highest point in all of the land and to his back was the Great Sea and all along the Lands of Man there was chaos. Below him the Black Machines were already chewing up the earth and any poor soul that got too close to them, the beasts anxious to be unleashed. The people of this Kingdom were gathering in force at the foot of the mountain and looking up into the trees as if waiting for someone or something to emerge. From what the Son saw of the smoke filling the air the same things were happening in the other Kingdoms that surrounded the Kingdom of Man. He knew that the Southernmost Kingdom used a form of magic that the rest of the Land had banned and there was a red glow that hung over that place. The Kingdom was led by a Warlock that had ruled for a hundred years, a King who had never stopped warring with the Kingdom of Man but who had lacked the courage to do more than pick, pick, pick at the borders like a bird at carrion. Within the Kingdom of Man something was happening as well. The Son could see deep black ruts were being carved into the land and these ruts resembled what the Black Machines did but there was smoke that came from that hovered like ground mist, so it was something else doing the damage. It seemed his sister had entered the fray as well. Good. This would make everything all the sweeter as the Queen's Kingdom fell. The Son had an itch though in the back of his mind that even all that he saw was not the full story, that there were other forces that were exerting their influence but on what and what it meant troubled him. These were powers too vast and great for him to be able to see and he didn't know what they wanted or why they were interested in what was happening but it worried him. Deeply.

Whatever was coming though, let it come. LET IT COME.

This was his time.

This was his destiny.

His inheritance.

Even in his dreams he had thought of this time, of this moment, at the edge of battle and anxious for the moment when he could stand upon the bodies of his enemies. Many, many years earlier, after he had killed the farmer, he and his men had been heading for this land to sow the seeds of war and strife and to see what mischief they might get into and then suddenly everything turned white, then black, and he awoke centuries later, his body buried in a shallow grave he had dug with his hands to get away from the fire and his men no more than dust. He did not know what had happened to him, what witchcraft had befallen him but he understood very well the power of the Queens of the Kingdom of Man and knew that his Mother had made enemies of them and had fallen prey to the Pandas as he slumbered but soon, very soon he would clear the ledger and make all Kingdoms fall before him before they were burned to nothingness. He would not stop until this world was ash and only he, his sister, and the fire remained and then only the fire.

Let the fire take it all.

And let his father find him there.

The Son came from a marriage between Lady Hush and a thing of pure fire she had found hidden in a cave deep within the Thicket and with his mother gone and the fire thing long absent he wished nothing more than to seek out his father in the flames themselves, hoping they might one day be reunited. He had always loved his mother and always would but even in her love for he and his sister she was cold. Obsessed with war and death. Obsessed with dying. It was so much for them. He had been the favored one, his sister more creature than anything else had been pushed into the shadows yet it was his father he had always felt closest to. The father he had never known. He had seen his father in dreams but his father said that mother did not want him in his life, just as she didn't want the father of his sister in her life, he a thing made of darkness and shadow. No, mother was all they would have. Mother. And over the years had had come to hate her for that and the hate and love were always at odds, always at war but the love forever won out. In the years of his childhood it was the flame that was his only comfort. It was there that he hoped to find his father. There had been another voice in his head as he slept a voice that came before his mother, a voice he didn't recognize but which promised him salvation if he would serve. Promised him an end to the pain if he would follow. Promised to punish the entire world if he would do as he was asked. The voice called itself Loneliness but it was drowned out by the voice of his mother and so he never was able to learn more. Maybe, he hoped, maybe if he waged this war, burned this world, maybe then his mother would let him go, maybe his father would find him again, and maybe the other voice would do as it promised and end the aching pain of loneliness he felt deep in his heart.

The Son heard voices approaching and shook his head to clear the memories and turned his attention to the four men and old woman coming up the hill towards him. The Son suddenly realized he had been crying and quickly wiped the tears away with a tattered sleeve and stood straight, pulling his robes around him as he did. He had never been a King before so he wasn't sure how to look or what to say so he stood shifting his weight from one foot to the other, smiling then frowning then smiling and flailing his scepter back and forth as if he was casting for butterbugs. Finally, as the small group crested the hill he moved to his throne and dropped into it, letting his robes fall in heaps at his feet as he leaned forward with anticipation, the crown cocked to one side and the Son's face dark and unsmiling. The people quickly topped the hill and, on seeing the Son they looked down at their feet and were silent. The silence spread outward and the Son shifted in his seat, waiting for them to say it. It was the youngest of them, a man no older than twenty who spoke.

"Welcome friends to my humble home, how can I help you?" He asked with a thin smile.

"Are you the man from our dreams?" Asked the youngest of the men.

"What is it you are asking, sir?" Not angry but wanting them to say it, to admit it.

"Are...we..." Said another of the men.

"We come because you are to lead us. You are the King that was sent here to lead us against our enemies and we have come here to ask you to do just that – to lead us. Our King has left us weak and we ask you, no we *beg* you to lead us and our Black Machines to war against our enemies" It was the old woman who spoke now, looking the Son in the eyes without any fear, her own face withered with time and scarred by the past.

The Son straightened and stood, the sight of his burned features making the group, all but the woman, step away from him while the flames of his robes that pushed them all back another two steps. He straightened his crown and lifted his scepter and pointed it at them.

"And will you die for me?"

"We will die for our Kingdom." Said a man whose face was more beard than skin.

"That is good enough. Tell your people I am coming and ready your machines. I will come at dawn tomorrow and when I come down the mountain...there is no stopping this. Prepare yourselves. We are at war."

The people stood awkwardly and in a heavy silence until the youngest bowed and then the men bowed and the old woman curtsied and then they all went slowly back down the way they had come, talking amongst themselves in low tones. He could hear them until they were almost down the mountain and smiled to hear their talk. They feared him. Even if it was just his burned features they still feared him and by the time dawn came all of them would fear him and there would already be legends about who he was and *what* he was. He sat carefully on his throne, his body aching from the burns, which made it hard to walk without wincing. He closed his eyes and thought of fire, still trying to calm down from the excitement of what had just happened. King. They had called him King.

He forced a smile that fell to a wince as pain crisscrossed his face and listened to the voices fade, the coughing fade, and the sweet sound of the fire to come as it roared across the world and left only ash behind.

Dawn couldn't come soon enough.

X

It was the first dream Messy had had in months that wasn't a nightmare. She had had dreams of fire and ash and screams that only got worse and more vivid and it became that she could scarcely sleep anymore. Messy would spend most nights lying in bed and staring off into the darkness watching as the Kreep Sheeps crossed in front of the moon. Even her Meep Sheep couldn't bring a smile to her face that would last more than a moment. She was inconsolable and with Vix gone so often she was left alone with her thoughts, which were cloudy. The Queen had been struggling with a problem that she could find no answer to – *what came next?* Something was coming, that was clear, though the voice of the past Queens no longer came to her she still could feel them speaking and knew that they were saying *something*. Warning her. Something was coming.

So she could run...but she wouldn't run.

She could fight...but she wouldn't fight.

So what was left?

Something...else.

Things had gotten so bad of late that even her Art, the one thing she felt she could rely on when times were darkest, had left her. Everything she started she never finished anymore. Nothing was good enough. Instead of relaxing her the struggles with her Art just made her more anxious and upset. There had to be an answer somewhere of what she needed to do.

Then the dream.

In the dream she saw the world on fire, the landscape turned to ash, just as it had been in every other dream. The Kingdom, the world was gone. Tears came to Messy's eyes and she fell to her knees in the ash and pushed her hands into it and brought up fistfuls. The other dreams she had fought the tears, had fought to be strong but not now, not now, no, she left the tears come, let them come and fall into the remnants of all she had known and loved. As the tears ran down her face they began to fall into the ash and with each tear that fell a blade of emerald colored grass grew and as she watched first a few, then a dozen blades rose out of the earth. In moments the grass had spread first two then five, then a dozen stones all around the Queen and as more tears fell more grass grew and the farther it stretched and beneath her she felt the ground shake and saw in the distance that trees were beginning to sprout up out of the grass. Messy stood and where she had knelt quickly turned from ash to grass and all around her the world was being reborn, the signs of the war being overtaken by new growth and new life. Messy opened her mouth and out flew a dozen butterbugs which flickered with light. She was scared, scared but excited too because even here, in this wasteland there had been hope, life, waiting to be released. Messy felt someone take her hand and turned and saw her mother and her mother spoke to her and then was gone and the Queen was awake again.

"The Queen's Tears."

Messy smiled in the darkness and knew then, knew what she must do, what she was meant to do.

This was her answer.

The Queen's tears.

X

As the sky slowly disappeared word spread from village to village that people had seen great, horrible beasts crossing into the Kingdom of Man from the East and destroying everything they came across. These monsters ate everything in their path and had already laid waste to three villages. Others talked of trouble with the Thicket and that Ashley had abandoned his post and the woods had gown wild. There was talk of the neighboring Kingdoms declaring war on the Kingdom of Man and some said that Lady Hush was back to get revenge on them. There were a dozen stories and none of them saw the full picture, only pieces of the whole. What everyone seemed to agree on though was that the Queen had gone mad and had abandoned them.

As the sun set a man and woman were arguing as they crossed a barren field on an abandoned farm that some called haunted. They were on their way from her parents' home in the town of Yon and back to their home in Larren, both of them desperate to be home where they could lock the doors and arm themselves with items the wife's mother had given them.

"It's time to run." He whispered.

"Yes, it's time to run, before it's too late." She replied.

"Maybe it already is too late. And who would take us? Where would we even go? Where is there to go?"

"Away, we just go away. Perhaps to the sea." She grabbed his hand and squeezed it.

"Nooooooooooo." Whispered a third voice.

The couple stopped walking and looked around and saw no one. Nothing. The field was barren save for a large, dark willow tree which hung limp and still even in the slight breeze that blew. The woman clenched her husband's hand tighter and they began to walk again, this time very slowly, hoping they had both heard the wind, or an animal, or nothing at all.

"No, you don't leave. You *never* just leave." Said the voice.

The man, deciding that someone was playing a prank on them spun around and said in a loud voice –

"Oh, and what does one *DO* then?"

"You fight. You fight for what you love and who you love. There are times to run, but this is not such a time. You must fight. Sometimes fighting for what you love means saying nothing, swallowing words like they are nails that want nothing more than to get out, but sometimes, sometimes it means standing your ground and screaming at the top of your longs *NO!*" There was a loud crack and the tree turned, shifted, and rose from the ground, pulling itself out of the dead soil and stretched its long branches as if it had not moved in a great while. After it stretched it leaned towards the couple, who were shaking with fear.

 "You fight. You fight because this is your Kingdom, these are your people, and this is your home. You fight because it's better that than to forever be running from the things you fear and the people who wield that fear."

 The voice was that of a woman and it came from the great tree before the couple and suddenly the woman realized where they were and what the tree was – the Weeping Willow. The husband recoiled from the tree, pulling away from his wife and taking step after step after step away. His wife turned and shot him a look of pure disgust and turned back to the tree.

"He's afraid. *We're* afraid."

"I know, but I can tell you that it is better to feel fear and act than live in fear and do nothing and the path you stand on forks only two ways and the choice is yours alone to make."

The Widow cracked her branches one more time then turned from the couple and began moving slowly towards the far forest, its roots moving like tentacles to pull it across the barren ground. The woman opened her mouth to ask one last question but closed it and turned back to her husband who was shaking. She had never seen him so scared in all of their thirty three years together and her heart sank to know what he would say before he said it and suddenly her own path seemed to veer from his.

"Ok…" He said.

She was silent.

"Let's go home. We have to get ready. Constable Klevins is forming a militia. They are going to start preparing the town tomorrow morning so there is still time to get home and sleep a few hours before we can join them."

The woman's mouth dropped open and she ran to him and embraced him and they both began crying. The man watched the Widow over his wife's shoulder as they embraced as the large tree approached then disappeared into the woods and closed his eyes against the world and was happy to have this last moment of peace

X

The Palace was abuzz as news spread of armies gathering in the neighboring Kingdoms. Scouts that had been sent had never returned and even some Pandas had disappeared when they went to investigate. It was only word of mouth from the nearby villagers that helped to inform the people of the Kingdom. As desperate as things we becoming the people of the Kingdom seemed to have two options – run or fight. As the full moon rose over all only a sliver of it was visible to those far below as smoke covered the rest of the night's sky and threatened to swallow the last remaining bite by morning.

Away from everything, far up in her room sat Aribel, content to be in the darkness with her thoughts and her writing. The voice in her head had become like a headache that wouldn't go away and the only thing that would dull it was when she was able to concentrate on working on a song or poem. Within the Palace the servants and staff were becoming anxious. No one had seen the Queen in over a day and even the King seemed preoccupied. Things were spinning out of control. Ari wanted to help, desperately wanted to help but wasn't sure how so she sat in the darkness and thought, and thought, and thought and waited to see what would shake loose in her mind.

In her own room Beliar played with two purple flames that she directed to slither up and down her thin, sleeveless arms. The flames snaked up one arm to her shoulder around the back of her neck and down the other arm to her wrist, twins that would meet in the middle for a moment and form a ball before switching sides. Beli didn't like to do magic around others. She didn't trust people and from the looks she got they didn't seem to trust her either. After what had happened in the woods Arnk and Aribel had treated her differently and for a long while Ari had been distant but since the girls had begun their formal training to become Mistresses of Magic and Queens they had started to bond again and were getting closer than they had been since they were little girls. Since the day they realized that they were different, that they were not Ari-Beli, two parts of one heart, but Aribel and Beliar, two girls sharing one life, the sisters had drifted apart. Once they had both walked hand in hand through the mud and then through a patch of Sigh-Boughs, flowers that would sigh and change color every time something touched them, the two of them on their way to swim in a nearby pond but a day came when a teacher teaching them about art looked at what both produced and began to favor Beliar and the same happened with the Science teacher when they looked at what Aribel was doing and fawned over her and started to give her different projects and that was when the divide between them began. A divide that became a gulf and then Beli began sneaking out at night to go see the Carnival boys when they were in town or to go talk to the wash-girls in the nearby village, or just to go and make things with her magic while Ari would sit in her room and watch her sister, not wanting to get into trouble herself but jealous for all that Beli was doing. Sure, Beli could draw, she could write, she could sort of make things out of clay but it was all just dressing to distract from what she loved and that was to make things out of magic. She loved to build places and things and even people out of light and stone and mud. She would never breathe life into the things, would never cross the line that was so clear in her but she wanted to. Beliar felt her power, felt it waiting to get out and to be set free but she pushed it back down, afraid of it. Afraid of what it could do. What she could become. Remembering what had happened in the Umwood and what she had made. Both beautiful and frightening.

When she was fifteen there had been a boy that Beli had liked, had maybe loved, and he had been the first boy she had ever kissed but she had found out that he had only spoken to her because he found out she was one of the Princesses and afterwards had told his friends that she definitely didn't know magic if the kiss was anything to judge by. She had heard this from one of the wash-girls and any tears she had felt were burned from her face as a nasty smile crossed her lips. That night she had taken a ribbon he had given her and had taken it and had snuck out and had made a fire, which she threw the ribbon into. When the fire had burned out she took the ashes and formed them into a hideous little creature which she then put a black spark of life into. A spark that ignited the thing and brought it to terrible life and with no word from her the thing set out for the village and the boy and she immediately regretted making the thing because she knew it came from the darkest part of her heart and she was afraid of what it would do. It was gone less than five minutes before she was off and running after it, feet pounding against the ground until she came to the cottage of the boy's family just in time to see the little creature erupt into flames in the living room of the home. Luckily someone inside saw the flames and was able to get everyone out safely but the home was a total loss. Beliar hid in the shadows of the trees nearby and watched the house burn and nearly screamed when she felt a tug at her nightgown and turned to see the thing standing beside her, a crooked smile cutting into its blank face as the heat from the fire came off of it in waves. It smiled at her, waiting more instructions and that moment all of the fire and hatred in her bubbled forth and as this boy she'd only known for a week's home burned her own heart burned into an inferno and she thrust her hand into the things chest and grabbed something and pulled it free. Out of the thing came the ribbon the boy had given her and suddenly the small thing went limp and it stopped moving and was still. Beli looked down at the ribbon in her hand and saw it start to smolder then catch fire and disappear and in her heart the inferno blazed and part of her, part of her wanted to dance in the ashes that were forming behind her because he deserved it, even if she was wrong, even if he didn't deserve it he DESERVED IT and that was why she stopped doing magic for many months afterward and focused her attentions on the other arts. Focused on quelling the blaze within before it consumed her.

Slowly, slowly the fire within Beli died down and she began to feel herself again and she hid it all away and the Kreep Sheep which had become her friends in her isolation, stopped coming to her as often and she felt so alone, so completely alone. In that loneliness though Aribel and she started to talk again, started to laugh again, and started, slowly, to become friends. But the darkness was there in Beli always waiting to get out but always in check as she walked the line between who she feared she was and who she wanted to be.

Beliar clenched her fists and the fire snakes disappeared and she was alone in the darkness. She closed her eyes and could hear everyone talking in the Palace and she felt the fear she'd been pushing down rising in her, slowly rising and as it did so too did the flames in her heart and she let them rise. Something had taken Aribel and had tried to lead Beliar somewhere dark, a place of dark magic and dark stories. A dangerous and hungry place. This was more than a war that was coming, this was something else. The Kreep Sheep could sense it. That was why they had stopped coming around as often. They were gathering near the Thicket. She wasn't sure why but she knew that they knew and that something was about to change.

Beliar had run from the darkness in her for so long it was time to embrace it. To use it. She had run from it and in turn had run from herself. It was time to let the darkness come. It was her Art, her true Art, and it was time to use to make something beautiful.

Something beautiful and terrifying.

X

Aribel had always been the good girl. The normal girl. The golden girl. She hated it. She hated that Beliar was so much like their mother. She was dark and moody and everyone said she looked just like their mother. She hated that Beliar could do things with magic that Ari had dreamed of doing but couldn't and if what everyone said was true Beli was a true Mistress of Magic. And what did that make Ari? She didn't know. She had her art, her writing, and she loved it, loved it dearly but it wasn't magic. It wasn't special. It was just something she did. She didn't feel magic inside of her. Not at all. She didn't feel anything like that. She felt like a lie. She felt so jealous of her sister that when Beli had saved them in the forest when that thing attacked it was all she could do to look her in the face. She was ashamed that she hadn't been able to do anything. She acted as if she feared Beli but the truth was that she envied her the power she wielded. And what could she do?

Nothing.

Aribel poured herself into her studies and her writing and focused all of her energy on those things. She had never had many friends outside of her sister and she withdrew from the ones she had and would watch from her window as Beli would sneak out and away. Oh how Ari envied her sister's daring and bravado. Maybe it was the magic that gave her that wild streak. Or maybe it was something else. Something Aribel would never have. When, after so very long Beli came to Ari crying one night, crying to her and smelling of smoke she knew things would be different. They didn't speak for weeks after that night and when Ari asked her sister about it Beli became strange and quiet but afterwards they slowly became closer again. Ari never lost the feeling that there was always something missing inside her though. That she was holding herself back. She would stay up nights, well after her studies were done and would practice magic and could only manage the most rudimentary of spells or events, as her teacher called them. She could do a few things Beli couldn't but they didn't amount to much in her own mind. Just tricks and not real magic.

So if she wasn't magic, like her mother and sister what was she?

She wished she knew.

Ari sat at the window as dawn neared; dressed because of a dream she had where something was speaking to her, telling her it was time, a gentle voice, a voice from the forest it said. It wasn't harsh and demanding as the other voice had been. In fact that voice was pushed out completely by this new one and she felt calm and warm as it spoke to her. It told her to rise so she rose and dressed and here she sat, watching as the sky faded to gray and as she watched she saw her father appear and walk from the Palace to the edge of the terrace below where he looked up to the sky and seeing him Ari knew that this was her moment. This was her cue. She rose and grabbed her boots and pulled them on and tied them.

She had never seen her father in his armor and if he was in his armor then it was as everyone said – it was war.

And this was her time.

X

Vix watched as the dawn came then disappeared; the smoke from the other Kingdoms blotting out the sun and sending the world into a hazy gloom. The smell of smoke and fire was getting stronger by the day and there were already reports of violence to the North and talk was that the other Kingdoms would invade when the sky was fully dark. That meant today. That meant now. Vix took his eyes from the sky and looked out over the rolling hills where animals and children were playing just weeks earlier and which were empty now. People weren't coming outside now. Many were leaving altogether, taking only the necessities and leaving the rest behind. His people were fleeing for their lives, afraid of a war they had no part in setting in motion and had no hope of halting without bloodshed. And that was the image Vix kept in his mind as he dressed in his armor – the people leaving their lives behind out of fear. That was what had made Vix bring the armor out of its trunk, the armor of his father and his father's father, knowing that his family, his people, and his land depended on him now. Messy had held things up for so long, had held the burden of keeping the sun shining as much as she could either directly or through the Meep Sheep and atop that had had a family to take care of and a Kingdom to oversee and the burden had become too great.

She had lost her joy.

Her hair had lost its colors.

She had lost her smile.

And he had been gone too much.

    Vix had always known the day would come when he'd be forced to choose – his home or his Kingdom. He had known and always pushed it off until he had no choice. It had taken a regent to come to him, begging forgiveness for being so forthright with him but telling him that it was time for him to let go of the crown. Vix hadn't gotten angry at the time but had suddenly felt a deep relief that someone had finally made the choice for him. It was time to go. It was time to hand things to someone else. Someone who could be there. Someone who was meant to stay. That had begun the search but it had been a short one. Once he had heard someone talking about Glen, who had the voice as clean and sweet as fresh rain, he started to remember stories of the Song Fathers and how some had left to chase music across the seas. Once he had met Glen and had heard him sing he knew who his successor must be and just one look at the stone in the walking stick Vix carried confirmed it. The stick was known as the Father's Burden and was what the Carnival King had to show who he was, instead of wearing a customary crown, which was worn only when visiting other Kingdoms or during special ceremonies. Set into the top of the Father's Burden was a stone that had been part of the Song Hall that had been a hall for the Song Fathers in the time before Kingdoms but there had come a war and the building had been destroyed. The hall had become illuminated whenever a Song Father came near, imbued with an old, lost magic, and it was discovered that the stones still lit up when near a Father and the stone did just that around Glen. But finding Glen wasn't the hard part, getting him to understand who he was, what he was, and what he could do was the hard part. And it had taken weeks to do this and then more time to prepare the Kingdom for his arrival and the exchange of power. Messy would never understand that his Kingdom had never, *never* lost a King before old age. Had never had one step aside. Had never had one just walk away? Many saw the Carnival Kingdom as something light and silly but they were a proud people that were tightly knit because of their constant travels and were close because of the work they did, which was inherently magical. The people of the Kingdom knew that Vix was married to a Queen across the sea but the thought had always been that she would come to their land one day and abdicate her thrown and not the other way around. Things had gotten tense in the Carnival Kingdom and Vix had heard there had been some protests when the news got out about his leaving and some questioned whether he should return to hand off the crown and Father's Burden but he insisted.

And there had been tears.

And there had been boos.

And there had been angry shouts and protests but he went and he honored his father, and the throne, and spoke to the people of his love for the Kingdom, for the Carnival, for his people, and for the crown but that no matter how much he loved all those things his heart belonged somewhere else. In the end he had handed Glen the power and had left as a beloved son of the Kingdom, and had crowds line up to hug him before he left. As soon as he stepped foot onto the boat that brought him back to his wife and daughter's a part of his heart was lost to him forever but another part, a larger part, finally became his once more.

From behind Vix came the sound of someone clearing their throat and he knew without turning who it was.

"Thank you for coming, Arnk."

Vix didn't turn but knew his old friend preferred he not. Arnk had been horribly scarred during a battle along the sea that Messy never knew about, a battle where Vix would have died. Arnk had taken the brunt of the attack and had not been the same since, stepping down from his role of protecting the girls and taking to the life of a monk. He still wrote to Vix but he didn't like to see people and the relationship between the two was forever different. For the girls it was worse because they had lost not a guard but a friend. A dear friend. Vix had told the girls he was too ill to see anyone and Arnk would send notes to the girls with the letters he sent to Vix but everything was different now. Arnk had lost almost everything to save his friend but there was one last favor the King needed before he returned to that life once more.

"You know I could not say no to my King. I am honor bound, even now." Arnk replied.

"Yes, and I have taken advantage of this pledge of honor you have made to the crown and I apologize. You have been too good to me but I need this one last favor. I am ashamed but I have no choice. I am sorry." Vix lowered his head and felt tears bite at the corners of his eyes.

"You should never feel ashamed, my friend, never. Not with me. I know all too well what is at stake and understand that you must act as a King now, not as a friend. And I must serve my King, and not just my friend. As your friend and as your servant I have spoken to the Great Loof." Arnk told his friend.

"You what? He, he..." Vix turned to face his friend, forgetting politeness in his surprise. Arnk took two steps away from his friend, seeking a shadow when all was shadow now.

"He...he has returned to power. He looks better than I have seen him in many years. It is clear that he is approaching the end of his path but he has returned to the throne and he and his people are ready to stand with you."

"I, I..." Vix turned away again and felt a heaviness that was beyond the war. The weight of a people who were not his to lead into war.

"Now, not all of them want this. This is very controversial. Many have left in protest and are headed for the Thicket, to return to the tree that was their first home, but that was expected. The rest will stand with you. This is not you're your land, it is their land as well and the Panda Kingdom will not suffer watching idly by as their home is invaded. Gloof will meet you North of here at Mid-Day. You will have to take a Whisper Wagon to get there quickly. They will meet you just outside of Numa. It is thought that the enemy will be on the village before nightfall. You will make a stand there."

"That's fine. Fine. I can never thank you enough Arnk. You have suffered for me, for my family, and I release you. I release you from all duties. I release you to follow whatever path you choose." Vix turned once more to embrace his friend but found Arnk was already gone and he was alone. Vix looked up at the Palace and saw that the light in Messy's studio was on. She had been up all night again working. He dropped his head, shamed once more and slowly made his way towards the stables knowing he may never see his wife again.

"I'm coming with you." It was Aribel and he jumped a little to hear her voice.

"What? I…How are…I don't have time for

this. The answer is no, and that's final. Go back inside and look after your sister and mother."

"I wasn't asking. I am telling you. I am coming."

Vix turned and saw fierceness in his daughter that he had never seen. Her hair was wild and covered her eyes and he was glad for that. He had seen his wife like this and it was not something he liked facing.

"I...Please. Please, Aribel, you can't come. You just can't. I..."

"You need me. I don't know why but I know it. I know it in my heart. I have never asked you to believe me on anything before but please, *please* – I am coming with you. Trust me. *Believe* in me." Aribel pulled the hair out of her eyes and for a moment, one moment Vix saw someone, no, not someone, he saw people, women standing behind his daughter, women who glowed white and without understanding what was happening or why he nodded his acceptance to her and turned away from his daughter and began walking again.

Vix and Aribel rode towards the village of Numa, hand in hand in silence, both of them frightened about what they were heading towards but happy to be facing it together.

X

The Son strode down the mountain as dawn came on and he could hear the chatter of the crowds that had gathered to see who would lead them. He wanted the North Kingdom because that was the land where he had died and been reborn so in its way it was his home. The other Kingdoms his mother had directed in dreams. She had put puppet leaders in place, either religious for the Southern Kingdom, or military for the East and West and they were waiting for her command and would enter the Kingdom of Man and begin heading for the Palace.

The Palace must fall.

The crown must fall.

The *Queen* must fall.

As soon as the Son made it into the first clearing the crowd saw him and a startled cry ran through them and to this he smiled, though the smile was brief. Good. Let them fear him. With one hand he fanned out his robes, the flames singing the ground and leaving a trail of ash behind him. He headed for and mounted a large boulder that sat at the edge of the crowd and when he crested it he lifted his scepter high into the air.

"Friends, I am here. I have come from the high mountains with a heart of war and have come to lead you into battle. I have come to lead you to victory. I have come to burn. I do not ask you to love me and I do not ask you to worship me. I ask only that you to follow me and if you do I promise you victory and glory. Will you follow me?"

There was a moment of silence and the only sound was the churning of the machines that sat at the edge of the Kingdom but suddenly all the voices joined and a great roar shook the mountain, a roar that was echoed in the other three Kingdoms. Lady Hush whispered to her son – *Do not fail me.* The Son lifted his scepter once more then quickly lowered his arm and the Black Machines came to life and began chewing the earth again and broke the border and devoured the great stones that held it and there was no going back, it was war. Another cheer rang out. The Son stepped down from the rock and took his robe in his hands and shook it out and the forest behind him erupted in flames that spread quickly and clambered up the mountain. The Son marched forward and as he went the people parted before him and fell in behind him, walking through the ashes and clutching their knives, swords, axes, scythes, stones, and any other weapons they could find. As soon as the Son and the people of the Kingdom passed into the Kingdom of Man another cheer rang out and the thousands upon thousands of people spread out and walked in the muddy trail left by the Black Machines, ready to strike down any that opposed them never realizing that behind them their own lands were becoming an inferno, preparing the way for a new empire of ash.

X

To the South, to the East, and to the West the Kingdoms broke the old treaties and entered the Kingdom of Man. The South came with a small force of Warlocks that cracked the ground with magic and turned anyone foolish enough to stand against them to stone. The East set loose the three Blurrgs they had bred over the past few months from ancient eggs and these beasts fed well on the people of the Kingdom of Man and behind them came the small army of that Kingdom. And finally the West used its vast military and its own fire weapons but found the people of the villages of the Western front up for the fight and so there was an immediate and nasty battle just at the border as three of the villages of the Kingdom of Man joined together with an elite fighting force sent in aid to the former King from the Carnival

Kingdom. As the fire, destruction and darkness spread wide across the land here was one place where the people would not run, would not hide, and would fight to save the Kingdom they loved and as they held the border, and held back the army from the West more and more people came to join them. The people fought with magic that pushed the invading army back, with music that called the trees to fight with them, and with any weapon they could find. Just as the West was making a final push using a great ramming weapon that threw people aside as if they were paper five War Pandas joined the fight and tore the machine apart. Seeing the Pandas many of the soldiers ran off or surrendered and suddenly the numbers fighting for the Queen rose and the Western army, heralded for their fighting prowess and strength in past wars fell before the impassioned blows of simple villagers refusing to yield and the brave souls that stood with them.

And so, but half a day into the Last War the West surrendered and its soldiers laid down their arms and its leaders cried out for mercy, for the Pandas not to invade their lands and slowly, so slowly the Western Kingdom all awoke from the nightmare of Lady Hush, who had willed them to war. She tried to force them to fight on but the sudden and overwhelming defeat at the hands of the enemy had loosened her control so she released the Kingdom but not before she willed one last person to set the fields to the West ablaze. If they would not fight for Hush then they would lose everything.

None could reach the Queen or the citadel in time to report what had happened in the West so it was Skraw, the daughter of Gloof, son of the Great Loof took command of the Western Front and told three of the War

Pandas and half of the villagers to remain while she took those from the Carnival Kingdom, two War Pandas, and the rest of the villagers to aid the Queen in the citadel. What shocked everyone though was how many soldiers from the West volunteered to go as well and to fight for the Queen. One hundred men and women from the West stood along with the rest and marched towards the Palace in the hopes they would not be too late.

X

Messy had been working for two days straight on her project and finally, finally it was complete. It was done. She stood and almost fell, her legs numb from being on the floor so long. She grabbed a nearby chair and pulled herself up and leaned on it as she looked down on what she'd made. It wasn't pretty but it was beautiful and was something that made her feel warmth to touch. It was right. It was exactly what it had to be. It was a small green box made of wood and carved with the image of a leaf but it wasn't the box that had been the work but what was within it and within it was the sum total of all of her magic. It was the culmination of all she knew and could create and she hoped it was enough. She hoped it was enough to make a difference. She stumbled to the window and looked out and let out a startled cry to see the sun gone and that there was heavy fog covering everything. She scanned the grounds of the Palace and saw no one then turned her attention to the nearby village and again, saw no one. She turned and looked at the clock on the wall and saw that it was mid-day but where were the people.

Beliar and a guard threw the door to the studio open and rushed to the Queen.

"Mother, what's wrong? We heard you cry out." Beliar took her mother's hand and looked into her face. "Mom, are you ok?"

"I'm fine. I'm fine. Where is everyone? I don't see anyone out there. Is there a celebration? Or a storm? Why wasn't I told there was a storm coming?"

"My Queen it's..."

"*Mom* it's not a storm. It's not a celebration. We've been invaded. We're at war."

Messy's eyes, which had been clouded, became instantly clear and she focused on her daughter.

"War? But we haven't been at war since before you were born. Since before I was Queen. I...but I knew, I knew it was coming but not yet, not yet. No, it...What happened?"

"I don't know. No one tells us anything. Dad left earlier. He was in armor. You need to get downstairs into the safe rooms below, you need to go now." Beliar grabbed her mother's hand and started to drag her towards the door but Messy pulled her hand free and took a step away from her.

"No. *No.* I will not run from this. I can't. I will stand and fight"

"Mom, you *can't*. This isn't like before. There's word that the Northern parts of the Kingdom are lost, rumors that there is trouble in the Thicket. This is bigger than anything you have faced before. You can't fight this battle. You can't."

Beli pleading now with her mother with tears in her eyes. She knew there was something wrong with her mother but now, now she feared that something was more than just wrong but that something was broken inside her.

"Guard, leave us, please." Messy asked.

The guard looked from Messy to Beliar and the Princess nodded and he turned and left the room, closing the door behind him.

"Beliar I know you think I am sick. I know that you all think I am sick. I know. Just as I know that I have been distant these past months and I can never make that up to you, to any of you. I have felt the weight of these past years as if they were stones upon my back and each year there was another stone added to the rest. It is nearly time for me to enter the Mother Wood and I know it. I know it and I am afraid. Afraid what my legacy will be with the Kingdom and with my family. And afraid of what comes next." Messy was crying now, the tears coursing down her cheeks as she leaned on the chair again. Beliar went to speak but Messy held her hand up to silence her.

"Please, please let me finish. I am afraid that I will be the Queen that created the Meep Sheeps and nothing more. And I adore them, and they are a part of me that they hope will always remain here and remain beloved but I want to feel as if I have left this Kingdom strong, and happy, as my Mother left it to me. In my sorrow I lost track of the land and now we are at war. War. My mother would never have let that happen. I should never have let that happen."

Beliar interrupted.

"Mom, Mother you don't understand. This is something more than just war. This is vendetta. This is revenge. I went to Arnk but he wouldn't see me, wouldn't speak to me, but he gave me a note and it read – *The Son and Daughter have returned to finish the Mother's work.* I don't know what that means but I remember what the thing in the woods called itself in my mind and that was Daughter and you know what its mother was, and if there is a Son and they are part of that family then mom this is so much more than just a war. You have to understand that if they catch you they will they hurt you, they will kill you and that would devastate the Kingdom and destroy your family." Beliar felt the tears at the corners of her eyes but they evaporated as soon as they hit her cheeks, as the fire in her began flare up.

"But don't you see Beli that if I run away and let these invaders take our nation and harm our people that our Kingdom will already be lost? If a Queen is not willing to stand beside her people in the worst of times then she has no right to stand with them at the best times. We must face them. We must face them and stand against them but do not think we stand naked, there is yet a fire and fight in me, my sweet." This time it was Messy's turn to take her daughter's hands. Beliar pulled her hands free and threw her arms around her mother, sobbing.

"Then I am going with you. Nothing you can say will stop me."

Messy hugged her daughter tight and nodded.

"As soon as you came in I knew I had no choice. I knew you would come with me. What about Ari though?"

Beli pulled away from her mother.

"I can't find her. I don't know where she is."

"Then maybe it's time we found out." Messy

said, though before she could make it to her dresser where a Seeing Stone sat next to the Dreamer's Dance orb her mother had given her the guard stepped back into the room.

"Your majesty I have grave news, Lady Aribel is gone. One of the staff saw her leave with the King. We couldn't stop them before they left. I am sorry madam. The young woman who watched her go knocked at your door, I heard her doing it myself but you never answered. I am sorry."

Messy dropped her head a moment and felt another stone fall upon her back. She had let her family down so many times. So many.

"Your Majesty it isn't for me to say, and I beg your pardon, but the King would never allow your daughter to go if he didn't think he could protect her and for what it's worth I saw a regiment of War Pandas and those magic ones they have heading North a few hours back, the same direction the King and Princess were heading. I know that doesn't ease what you are feeling but I hope that will at least ease your mind."

"Thank you, I do appreciate that. Vix would never let harm come to her and he must have thought she could help and I guess I am lucky to have Beliar here to help me. Guard, will you see who is left here and tell them to go to the cellars, to the tunnels, not the safe room but the tunnels, and to leave the citadel. Tell them it is by order of the Queen, please, then follow them down there and lock the doors." Messy turned and looked out the window and in the distance saw the glow of fire.

"Your Majesty, begging your pardon, we've all agreed that wherever you go we shall follow. The guard will not leave your side. Any people left in the citadel are safely tucked away or are waiting for the order to fight. The people have made up their minds." The guard dropped to one knee and lowered his head. Messy turned back to him and smiled.

"Thank you, Garth. Please tell the others then that we shall head to the courtyard directly."

The guard stood, a shocked look on his face.

"I didn't know you knew my name, your Majesty."

"I have always known all of the names of the people who serve the crown but even the Queen must follow some protocol."

Garth bowed and quickly left and Messy and Beliar were alone.

"Mother, what's this box on the ground?"

Messy bent and took the box in her hands

and lifted it gently.

"Even in the darkest night there comes a dawn. Even in the void there is hope. Come, we must dress and meet our guests…and see them on their way."

Messy looked at her daughter and while Beli felt the fire building inside her one look at her mother told her that it was she that was the more dangerous of the two of them and finally she returned her mother's smile.

Far above them a bell began to ring.

Once.

Twice.

A third and final time.

War had come.

X

Ashley Pickles stood at the top of the hill where he had spent more years of his life than he could even imagine - a place that had become a home to him and where his mother and father had even spent the last years of their life. To Ash the Thicket and the creatures within it were better friends than he could ever have asked for. Somehow though, in the time since he had left to see the Queen the Thicket had changed and was now a stranger to him. A dangerous stranger. He had returned with two Pandas, members of the same company that Skraw served in and they immediately stepped in front of Ash and drew their spears. The forest wood was black and there was an unnatural silence within it.

"Didn't you say that there were a number of your tribe that had come back here once the Great Loof sounded the War Horn? If that's the case where are they? Why don't we hear or see them?"

Ruk, the younger of the two brothers accompanying Ash spoke.

"Yes, there should be sign. Some sign. There is nothing."

"Not nothing, no. I smell…something. Something…old. Something sick." Said Oot, the other brother.

The three of them were silent and Ash stepped away from the Pandas and walked towards his hut. When he got within ten feet though he stopped cold and covered his mouth and spun away from what he had seen within his old home. He looked at the Pandas with horror and uncovered his mouth.

"I found your people. Or some of them.

They, they're...who would do such a thing? What has happened here? What happened?" Ash asked.

Ruk ran to the hut and dropped his spear and screamed.

"They are here, they are here, brother they are here!"

Oot ran to Ruk and looked inside the hut and seeing what lay within he took a step back in horror.

"But, that cannot be all of them so where are the rest of our people?"

From the Thicket came a voice none had heard before.

"Oh, they are in here, with us brothers. Do you wish to see them?"

Zum stepped from the Thicket and behind him came a thick, barbed vine that pierced the heart of Ruk. Oot let out a war cry and threw his spear at Zum but missed and struck another Panda instead who fell immediately. Two more vines erupted from the Thicket and wrapped themselves around Oot and dragged him kicking into the forest where he disappeared. Zum turned his attention to Ash and from the darkness of the Thicket came a large War Panda that strode towards the human quickly.

"Oh dear, it seems your friends couldn't stay, what a shame. No worries, I came to see you, not them." Zum said with a smile.

"What have you done? What have you unleashed?" Ash was shaking with fury, wracking is brain for what he might use to fight with.

"Oh, you have no idea what I have done, but you will know. Oh, you'll know. Wait until you see the beautiful rugs we've made from your precious kitties. Praw, fetch the human and let's take him into the Thicket to see his friends."

"NO! I will not have that witch within me. Do what you must do in the open air." Another voice, this time booming from the very forest itself.

Zum's smile dropped and so too did his shoulders as a snarl cut across his mouth. Praw stopped only a few feet from Ash and looked back at his master.

"As you wish. Praw, it seems Mr. Pickles will be saying his goodbyes here then. So be it."

Praw grabbed Ash and lifted him into the air and towards his mouth and suddenly Zum's smile returned.

X

Vix rode in silence with his daughter near the Northern border but as they neared the village that lay there it was clear from the thickening smoke and the fleeing people that whatever spell of foolishness the King had been under when he told his daughter she could come with him had made him make a grave error.

"Ari, honey, I need you to listen to me – When we reach our destination you are going to stay in the Whisper Wagon and go back to your mother and sister. This is no game. I…I need you to be there for your mother in case, in case something happens. In case we can't hold back whatever is coming."

Aribel listened to her father calmly, surprised he hadn't said something sooner but knowing he would tell her this, knowing he would tell her she couldn't come and knowing all too well what her own answer would be.

"Beli is with mother. They are safe. I can feel them. They are preparing to face the enemy just as we are. I don't know why I need to be here father but I *need* to be here. I don't have a choice. Dad, has nothing ever told you that in your heart something was right, that it was meant to be even when all sense and logic told you otherwise? Is there no magic in you just as there is no art in me?"

And he remembered how he had known Glen was the man he was looking for just on seeing him, had known it and for a moment, the briefest of moments thought he had heard his father whispering in his ear – *it is he!* And he smiled and looked at the young woman across from him, so much his daughter, her mother, but so much someone else as well and he knew instantly who it was she looked like and then the smiled died because he knew who it was who had been standing behind her and why he had let her come – Queen Anamare, and behind her had stood the other Queens. All of them.

"Daddy?" Aribel had seen his smile come and fade.

"If there is anything I have learned dear daughter it's that magic is everywhere, is everything, and even if we lose our belief in it it is still there, waiting for us when we are ready to believe once more. We are all full of magic just as we're all full of art, we just have to trust in ourselves and both will come to us when we are ready. Well, come on then, shall we see these devils back to the inferno from which they have come?"

Ari smile and leaned forward and hugged her father, the both of them laughing briefly when their armor clanked together. The laughter died as the Whisper Wagon stopped and they realized they were at their destination. Suddenly the reality of what was happening in the Kingdom was all too real.

The village of Numa was no more. What remained of the buildings were on fire and there were piles of clothes everywhere that Aribel turned her eyes from, knowing what they were without needing to see more. Just north of the village was a great black smoke that poured up from the earth and there was a terrible sound that reminded her of the sound when someone would chew with their mouth open, that sound of wet chewing always making her lose her own appetite when she heard it. All of a sudden Aribel questioned the wisdom of them being there when a voice came to her as a soft breeze saying – *This is where you belong. Dear Aribel this is your path.* Her fear fell away and she was the first out of the Wagon and she strode forward through the piles of clothes and rubble towards the smoke. She bore no weapons and would bear none, instead she made her way to a piece of crystal that had been forged in the citadel, forged for the Queen and given, one to each village, as a way to call for help. The crystal blinked red, the color for immediate need of help, help that had come too late but help that had finally come. Aribel pushed the pillar that held the crystal over and pulled the blinking crystal out of the dirt and it felt right in her hand. She turned and saw her father making his way to her, his firebow drawn and his sword on his hip. She could see in his face that he feared that they were not only too late for the initial battle but too late to push the enemy back when Gloof and a War Panda emerged from the darkness ahead, bloody and covered in soot.

"Whatever you believed this to be Vix, whatever any of us thought this was – we were wrong. This is so much worse." Gloof looked over to Aribel and he nodded to her and patted the War Panda on the arm.

"Come, things are dire but now that you are here, the fight has just begun, and look – you have brought reinforcements with you." Gloof pointed beyond Aribel and her father and they turned and saw dozens of villagers approaching, weapons raised.

"For the Queen!"

"For the King!"

"For the Princesses!"

"For the *Kingdom!*"

Vix turned back to his daughter and they both began walking towards Gloof and his companion and the darkness, the villagers behind them. In a moment they were all enveloped by the darkness but within it there was a light, a sickly green glow that filled but could not escape the gloom. Ari held the crystal out and saw that it was casting not the red light but a bright white light that penetrated the blackness and cast it aside. She followed the light of the crystal deeper, towards the green glow and she thought she heard screams thought she heard cries but she wasn't sure over the sound of the chewing and gnawing that came on as thick as the darkness. The light ahead slowly got brighter and brighter and brighter and Ari barely noticed the things that flashed by her, that brushed by her, that pushed past her or the way the ground went from grass to dirt to mud, to muck. She was focused on the light and finally she was there and the light was brilliant, flooding everything and casting shadows that stretched and twisted and she realized that she was talking to herself, urging herself on only the voice that came out of her mouth wasn't her own. It wasn't her voice at all but the voice of a woman, an old woman and suddenly she realized with growing horror that she had been lead her. She heard laughter in her head and it was the voice from before that had come to her in so many dreams. It was a trap. She spun around saw she was alone here, her father and the Pandas and the villagers all gone. She was alone. She screamed and the voice of the old woman rose and rose and rose and cracked and Ari's own voice broke through and erupted from the darkness and pushed it back revealing the horror at the heart of the Northern front.

 The Daughter stood before her, bowed before the Princess and let the young woman see the things of the Void that surrounded them as they devoured everything in their path. Things part spider and part elephant pulled trees from the ground with their trunks then fed them into vast maws that took the trees in whole. Nearer to Aribel were things that were part hippo and part crab that grabbed any stray villagers that had wandered into and gotten lost and took those people into the fog. Aribel couldn't focus on the attacking things, there were so many of them, all of them towering over her but going around her and she knew why in an instant. This was the Daughter that stood before her and Aribel was hers. For one moment all was still and Aribel was flooded with fear but before she could run, before she could even scream there was a cool breath against her ear and the reassuring voice again – *Always fight Darkness with Light* – and all of a sudden the fear was gone and the only thing there was for her to fight was darkness.

    Aribel smiled at the Daughter and it hissed at her and rose to its full height, its maw opening wide as it ran at Ari with all it had. Darkness rolled out of the Daughter's mouth in a thick wave and suddenly Ari could see nothing. She fell to one knee and put a hand against the ground. It was hard to get a fix on anything, there was just too much chaos but there was something about the way the Daughter moved that set it apart. It was tentative, like a spider but one of its legs was useless, the one in the back. Something had happened to it after what had happened in Umwood and it gave the monster away. Ari closed her eyes and let the things brush past her, push past her, roar past her knowing her father and the others were waiting. And in the darkness of her mind she caught it, the slow, deliberate dance of the Daughter as it circled closer and closer and closer. Ari opened her eyes and heard a hiss and rolled to her right as a wooden spider leg barbed with poisoned hooks swung out at her. Ari rolled again and again and again as another blow and another and a third fell, all coming close but missing her. Ari got her feet beneath her and clenched the crystal as tightly as she could and leapt at the Daughter, swinging as she did. She felt the air around her explode with motion as the monster struck out and missed again but Ari didn't miss, swinging the crystal downward and connecting solidly with the Daughter and as she did the darkness was broken by brilliant white light that made the thing howl. Ari landed on her feet and in the brief burst of light saw the monster and the white fire that was burning it but the light faded and before the Princess could land another blow one of the legs sprang out and knocked her to the ground, forcing the air from her lungs. The world went red as soon as Ari hit the muck of the ground and the crystal slipped from her grasp. In a moment the darkness was back though and with it was the Daughter, who pushed its face towards Ari and opened wide its mouth.

Ari opened her mouth to scream but

couldn't get anything out as she realized she was sinking into the mud and her mouth was full of it. She shook her head to clear it but the smoke from the Daughter poured over her and into her lungs and all fight drained from her and the white light left her head and in its place was the screaming of the Daughter. Ari tried to force herself up but felt the weight of one of the Daughter's legs on her, pushing her deeper into the muck. Mud washed over Ari's face and the armor felt like it was made of stone. Ari raised her arms up and beat at the monster above her and was repulsed by the wet, soft feel of its skin, as if it was made of rotting bark. Touching it burned her hands but she knew she didn't have long before she was lost within the ground and had to try to get the thing off of her. It was useless fighting though and within moments her arms were like two pieces of lead and she dropped them and felt unconsciousness begin to swallow her.

There was a moment of weightlessness and in it she could see everything -herself, the Daughter, the burning forest around them, the massing armies that had surrounded the citadel and Palace, her mother and sister, and out and out and out and she saw the Thicket and great yellow shapes running towards the Thicket which shook and twisted on seeing these things and roared at them and Ari went outward further into the emptiness beyond where things became black and cold. But in that blackness there came a light and the light came from a ring of white trees and standing within that ring came the light, pouring from the most beautiful women Ari had ever seen and from the middle of the group came a woman that looked like her mother and her voice was familiar, so familiar.

Wake up.

Wake up.

Grandaughter…wake…UP!

"Wake up, Aribel, wake up. Please, please, you have to wake up!"

Ari opened her eyes and saw her grandmother and more light than she thought she could stand but it didn't hurt to look at but took the ice and lead from her body. As consciousness flooded her body All Ari could do was smile.

"Ari, *Ari,* are you OK? Why are you smiling? What is happening?" The voice of her father now and his face over her, blood running from a deep cut in his forehead and from a cut on his lip but he seemed to be the source of light in the darkness that surrounded them.

"Dad? Dad, where are we? What's going on?"

"Honey I lost you. You ran ahead of us and before we could follow you those things came out of the fog and stopped us. There are so many. Every one that fell three would replace it. One of the War Pandas fell to those things and when Gloof when to help him he too fell. When Gloof fell before those things I dropped my sword and ran and ran and ran to find you and found that thing atop you and so I fired from the firebow again and again until it finally retreated from you. As soon as it was gone I was able to pull you out of the ground. I thought you were dead. I thought you were dead. I thought…" Vix pulled his daughter fully out of the mud and embraced her and squeezed her tears running down his face as the image of his daughter motionless in the mud blended with that of the image of his friend dead within a pile of other Pandas and humans.

There was so much. There was just so

much that her father had told her that Ari could say nothing, could only wrap her arms around her father and let her own tears come at the loss of Gloof, who she had known for her entire life. She closed her eyes and she could see the final moments. The War Panda with its great paws holding back the snapping jaws of one monstrous white thing as another came behind and stung him with a long blade. The Panda fell before them and Gloof, seeing this, roared and ran to his friend, swinging a long sword and the white beast fell beneath the blade but as Gloof spun around to take on the other enemy the ground opened beneath him and a worm came up and Gloof ran it through with his sword but with his attention filled a creature that was part scorpion and part gorilla stung him with its own blade. Gloof pulled the sword free of the worm and swung around and severed the scorpion-gorilla in two and then his shoulders slumped and he fell to his knees, he dropped his sword and finally the great warrior was still.

The darkness drew away and the light returned and Ari pulled away from her father and looked at him and in that moment they were not just father and daughter but were servants of the crown, of the people, and of the light itself. She reached into the mud and pulled the dead crystal free and as soon as she touched it it lit up with bright white light again and Vix grabbed his firebow and both of them stood and faced the darkness.

The noise of the battle died down and all was quiet as Vix and Aribel stood back to back to face it. Sensing and hearing nothing Ari went down to a knee again and put her hand into the mud as she had before and closed her eyes and concentrated and hidden beneath the darkness there was movement, as if many things were circling them around and around and then she felt it all stop and in that moment she opened her eyes and stood quickly.

"They're coming."

From the darkness erupted a dozen Pandas carrying spears and clubs, and among them came only two War Pandas, the rest having been lost to the things from the void. Behind the Pandas came humans, bruised, battered and their numbers greatly diminished but there to stand together with the King and Princess against the oncoming creatures. Even now, with all the horror they had seen, there was still a Kingdom. Ari motioned for the Pandas and the humans to hurry towards the center of the darkness, where her crystal held the dark at bay and as more were added to the circle the light grew brighter and the dark retreated further. And as the last of them gathered with Ari and Vix the darkness drew back enough to reveal hundreds of the beasts encircling all of them, ready to strike. The things from the void were the like none had seen in a hundred years and more. They were species of animals joined by magic of the darkest kind that had been exiled to nothingness because they were never meant to exist. To look upon them was to see a living nightmare and seeing them took the heart out of the fight of many. How could they defeat such things? How could they face them?

There was a moment where both sides only stood and looked at each other and the darkness pushed against the glow of the light that came from the crystal but could get no closer. Ari closed her eyes but everything remained, the people standing around her radiating with white light and the monsters with green light and deep in the heart of them was the wounded Daughter, radiating scarlet with rage and watching to see what came next.

It was an impatient War Panda that rushed forward first, roaring and heading for something part lion and part centipede. The Panda grabbed it by its neck and the middle of its back and lifted it up and roared again before breaking it in two. Everything became chaos. One of the Pandas nearest Ari shot a fireball at a group of the things and created a hole where five of them fell but were quickly replaced. The monsters rushed forward and the humans did the same and when they collided it sent off the most beautiful and awful light Ari had ever seen, burning her eyes and forcing her to look away. Still the sound was muffled in the darkness but moment by moment the battle grew more frenzied. The War Pandas rushed forward and broke a hole through the center of the things but before the rest of their brethren could rush forward to join them they were cut off and set upon by the monsters. Vix raised his firebow and shot several blasts into the monsters and dropped them one after another but still they came, came and fell one by one beneath his weapon. The people of the Kingdom formed around the King and raised their weapons against the monsters as they came forward, protecting him as he killed the things. Ari felt something behind her and spun around and pushed the crystal forward without looking and it hit and went into one of the monsters and its eyes got larger and larger the deeper the crystal sank into it. The monster suddenly glowed with white light then went limp and fell dead to the ground. Ari felt a cold chill cross her and felt the heaviest of weights on her heart to see the beast that had a mind, had a heart, and had breath in its lungs a moment before now still and gone and dead. Dead. But there came another and another and another and as if by instinct she raised the crystal and swung it like a sword and the things dropped silent and as she fought Ari felt her grandmother near and others, so many others standing with her and guiding her so that she struck before the monsters could strike her but out of nowhere she felt a sharp pain that struck like lightning and dropped her to her knees. She screamed at the intensity of it but saw nothing near so she turned in time to see the Daughter rising high above her father, who was on his knees before it and she struck him first with one leg then another then another then it grabbed him roughly and pulled him forward and sank its teeth into his neck and shoulders.

Ari rose quickly and swung the crystal wildly behind her as she limped to her father. Everything felt like it was in slow motion, the things crowding towards her but falling one by one as if they were nothing when the crystal came near them. She turned her attention from her father to the Daughter and it was watching her intently and as Ari neared it retreated a few steps. Ari fell to her knees, ignoring what might come and her full focus on her father again but as soon as she fell she was surrounded by Pandas and humans who took to defended her as she attended the King.

"Dad?"

Silence.

"Dad?"

More silence.

"*DAD?*"

Ari leaned forward and put her head to her father's chest and at first heard nothing. She put a hand to his mouth and it was cold but she thought she felt breath. She leaned away from him and he was gray and still. Ari looked past the battle and saw the Daughter retreat another step then another, its body low now and its head bowed. Ari closed her eyes and the Daughter was purple now, the rage that had fueled it fading and was it regretful?

Was it?

Ari opened her eyes and looked away from the Daughter and all around her the battle was raging and there were so many bodies falling around her, friends and foes and it was too much. It was all too much. Ari closed her eyes and looked again with her mind and saw no sign of the white spirits, no sign of her grandmother.

They were gone.

She was alone.

The world closed in and the darkness pressed closer and suddenly Ari was a little girl again, confused and lost and with nothing to offer, no weapon to fight with, just nothing. She looked at her father and his eyes were open and blinking slowly and locked on her.

"…magic…everywhere…in you…"

Magic is everywhere. Even in you.

And then everything was different and the world was moving again and the sound was back - screaming, yelling, and chaos. She hurt. She was hurt bad. There was poison coursing through her and she could feel it burning its way to her heart but she ignored it and looked at her right hand and saw that the crystal was flaming with light. She looked around her and saw her grandmother and the others and they were smiling at her. Ari whispered the names of her family – *Messy, Vix, Beliar, Aribel* – like a spell and felt her hand becoming warm as the heat of the crystal spread through her, spreading and igniting her she rose and lifted her arm as she did all the fighting stopped and all eyes were on her because as she stood the white fire moved down her arm and over her entire body and she had become a living flame. The white flame consumed her and burned the poison from her. She looked around and saw a rainbow of colors.

"You things of the void – *leave!* This is not your world. You do not belong here. For you this war is over. *Leave!* I offer you this one chance at amnesty. This once chance at forgiveness. Leave now or fall before us. **GO!**"

Ari turned around and around, the crystal held high over her head, the white flames coursing down her arm and across her body, the light of it flooding everything around her and tearing the darkness apart. The things roared and clamored but the fighting had stopped and all attention was upon her and now it was she that was the monster and the things recoiled from her, drawing back and back and back until the Daughter and Ari stood face to face again. The Daughter stood silent, its body drawn tightly together and its head low and Ari saw it but its colors were fading to a cold gray. It didn't want to be here. Aribel felt that. The thing had been forced here, pushed and cajoled by its mother. Poisoned by words and images and forced to fight a battle it had no interest in. It didn't want war. It wanted…it wanted…it wanted to never be alone again.

Ari's heart broke for the thing.

"Go. Go now, go back to the void and you will never be alone again. Go before it's too late."

Whispered to the Daughter as Ari held the fury of the white fire within her, the fire that was pushing to get out, that was screaming to obliterate everything made of darkness. The Daughter lowered itself even more and slowly began to back up foot by foot and as it did so too did the other things. The Daughter rose to its full height and stood there a moment then bowed low, as if to curtsy then it turned and chattered to the other things from the void and then it turned and slowly began to hobble back the way they had all come. The things all did as the Daughter had and made little bows and then turned and followed back towards their home. Several humans and the last War Panda started after the things but Ari crystal and all the darkness which had hung like a fog suddenly receded and now the true horror of the battle and the cost of it was revealed.

"There has been enough death and enough darkness. *ENOUGH!*"

"But the King? You allow those monsters to..." Came a voice from the crowd.

"Allow? *ALLOW?* As if it is my dominion to grant and destroy life? Look around us. I said *look around.* Hasn't there been enough death? Hasn't there been enough horror here? I will not add to what has been done here. Those things, those creatures..." Ari trailed off, knowing they couldn't understand, that they hadn't seen, they hadn't seen the light hidden within the things, the light hidden deep within the Daughter, hidden so deep that the things couldn't see it within themselves. They had all been lied to, fooled as so many others had been by Lady Hush. Ari had seen how the Daughter changed when it saw the light, how it had changed when it had bitten her father, how it had realized what it had done and what it was Aribel realized that all of them were capable of the same things, the same terrible things.

"Princess, what, what do we do then? What should we do?" A badly wounded Panda asked.

"We gather our wounded and we head for the citadel. This isn't over. Come on, we have to hurry."

The survivors all looked at her, beaten, bloody, and unsure of what to do. She looked at her arm saw it covered in flames. She shook her head from side to side and the flames lowered and died and the light in the crystal faded and she was just Ari again.

"I won't ask you to follow me. I can't. You've done enough. But please, please just help me get my father into the Whisper Wagon. Please."

Again there was only silence and she realized maybe she had become a monster as well. She knelt down and looked at her father and he was still breathing though his eyes were now closed. She ran a hand over his cheek and he was cold but she could still see the white light in him, though it was low, like a dying flame. Tears began to run down her face and she dropped the crystal and looked up and there was so much smoke in the air, so much fire in the Kingdom. She didn't know how they could stand a chance. Ari felt so much weight on her suddenly that she wasn't sure she would be able to stand. Then they came, the people of the Kingdom and the Pandas, picking up her father and gently carrying him to the Wagon and helping her up and escorting her to be with him while the rest gathered the wounded and through her tears there was so much light.

 So much light.

Ari looked up and smiled because far above them there was a break in the darkness and the sun was shining into the world again.

The Warlocks

They came from the South, the Warlocks in white. They came with gifts of perfumes and spices and toys made of the most exotic of woods and they came bearing magic. The Warlocks hid their faces from the people claiming that their skin was delicate due to their life in the South and while some mistrusted the Warlocks most welcome the strangers with open arms, the sheer novelty of visitors to the Kingdom enough reason to let them stay though it could be said, and was, that the gifts were the real reason. The Prince was fascinated by the magic of the Warlocks and the King, wanting to make his only child happy, invited the seven Warlocks to stay in the Castle. The Queen had died during the Creeping Gray and since her death the Prince had been inconsolable. Until the Warlocks came the King wondered if his son would ever laugh again and now, now the boy couldn't stop laughing.

The Warlocks were happy to stay in the castle, to amuse the boy and, as tensions at the borders mounted, to counsel the King in how things were down in the far, far South. You know, they told the King, there are certain spells, certain conjuring, and certain *stones* that could be used to stop the tensions at the border. The King was desperate for a way out of the conflict that would spare lives. Too many had been lost in the border wars a dozen years earlier and he loathed to think those days might return. So as the Warlocks gathered around the throne and told the King of the things that *they* could do to help he listened, he listened and unfortunately he believed.

When the tensions at the border were calmed by the Warlocks it wasn't just the King that listened when the Warlocks spoke but everyone. And when the Warlocks spoke the King acted. For many months things continued this way, with the Warlocks amusing the King, his court, his son, and all that came near. One day though the Prince took ill and when the Warlocks told the king it was the Creeping Gray the King offered anything, *anything* to the strangers if they could but save his son. The Warlocks gathered together and conferred amongst themselves and told the King that yes, yes they could do this thing for him but there was a price. A very high price.

The Warlocks would save the King's son but to do so meant that he must give them the power of the throne. He could remain the King but they would be the power, they would be the rulers. They would be the hands that guided the Kingdom back to glory, back as a power, back as a nation to be loved…and to be feared. The King, wracked with grief and fear for the life of his son never once questioned how it was that his son had caught a disease that none in the Kingdom had had since the loss of his wife, never once questioned why his son didn't show any of the signs of the sickness but was instead comatose in his bead, and never asked the Warlocks what it was they whispered over the boy every night before he would take a another turn for the worse. No, the King asked nothing but gave all.

"Yes. Anything."

That night the Prince was miraculously cured and awoke from his coma and the son, in his joy, never questioned how, or why, or what came next and so ended the true reign of the King.

This was an age of Warlocks and all who questioned them disappeared, all that opposed them fell, and suddenly there were statues in the likeness of the Council of the

Crown, their inspirations having left the nation while everyone slept. The King did not appear out anymore, nor did the Prince. Suddenly the King wanted the military expanded and the borders protected and the oldest child of every household was conscripted to the Crown's Brigade in case of war. This was not a request, this was a demand and to disobey it brought dire consequences.

This was the Age of Warlocks and an age of shadows.

PART THREE

The smoke had thickened in the citadel and as Messy and Beliar exited the Palace the grounds were full of frantic people preparing for what was approaching. Beliar was happy to see that the children were gone, hidden away or taken away and that all that were left were adults. As she was scanning the growing crowd of people she saw the face of the boy who had broken her heart so long ago and he was unloading a cart full of spears with some other boys from the nearby village. He caught her gaze and stopped what he was doing and bowed and as he did so did the other boys and Beli felt her cheeks flush with color as they did this then rose again. This wasn't the first time she had had someone bow but him doing it sent a jolt of electricity down her spine and she dropped her eyes and looked at the rest of the scene.

She had looked outside just before she had gone to see her mother she had noticed that the grounds were empty but now there were people everywhere as if the Carnival was in town. Just as she was thinking that she saw a troupe of people rushing in from the West dressed in the bright colors of the Carnival Kingdom. Messy had been speaking to three of the Palace Guard, listening to reports of supplies and updates on what was happening elsewhere when the Captain of the Carnival unit rushed forward. The three guardsmen went silent at the sight of this new arrival. The Captain bowed to the Queen, then to Beliar and Beli was struck by how beautiful and ornate his armor was, all of it seeming to glisten and sparkle which gave life to the etchings that covered every inch.

"Your Majesty, I come with aid and with news."

"Captain, I thank you for your news but

embrace you for your aid." Messy stepped forward and took the soldier into her arms and gave him a long hug before stepping back. Her hair was full of soot and her face was smudged with it but Beli had never seen her mother more beautiful and still regal despite the pants and loose shirt she wore, something meant only to wear out into the wilds. To Beli her mother had never looked more like a Queen. Beli shifted the green box in her hands, which had a weight within it that seemed to shift and radiate with heat.

"Your Majesty, I am Brin from the Carnival Kingdom. We have come to aid you against the invaders. Upon landing we joined the fight at the Western front where, with the brave work of your people and the Panda Kingdom we were able to break the army of the West and force them to submit. Many lives were lost, we alone lost twenty-three of our one hundred and ten soldiers but we were able to secure the Western front and have added to our force another three hundred."

"Who joined the fight in such numbers?"

"The soldiers of the West have joined us." Replied Brin.

Messy's jaw dropped open.

"I don't understand."

"Nor did we, your Majesty. It seems they started the invasion after they had been plagued with dreams and a sickness that ran rampant among their people. It drove them mad. They said a voice compelled them to come and burn the Palace to the ground and to kill you, Queen Messy. They went so far as to pull down the statues you had made for them and destroyed them. Somehow the spell they were under passed though as we forced them to submit or perish and they realized with horror what they'd done. Many of their soldiers joined us and we expect there will be more joining the fray later. I hope they won't be needed but they may. From what we have seen and heard, the North, South, and East are headed here in force. Your Majesty, it is going to get not just bad but ugly here. I know you feel an obligation to stay but…"

Messy interrupted Brin.

"There is no choice or question. I will stay." Messy looked to her daughter and smiled.

"*We* will stay. We will stay and fight."

Brin looked at Messy a moment and nodded, finally understanding what could lead his King to give up his crown and his Kingdom for this woman and her land.

"Then we must…"

A scream interrupted Brin and everyone spun around and saw three hideous monsters smash through the tree-line and take out thirty guards with swipes of their paws.

"What beasts are these?" Asked Brin.

And as if coming from a dream Messy answered.

"Blurrgs. From the East. We though, everyone thought...they are supposed to be extinct. Gone since the last wars." And the true horror of what was being unleashed came into full view for the Queen.

The Blurrgs swept away everything in their paths, trees, statues, and guards alike and then shook the ground with their roars. The three broke through the outer walls of the Palace's grounds together as if they were made of sticks and then divided and started crushing the defenses that ran to fight them.

To the South a horn was sounded and Beli turned and saw a flash of purple light and a moment later heard an explosion. As she was focused on what was happening on the south lawn she felt a hand on her wrist and she looked down at the hand and then up to her mother, who was looking to the North and Beliar followed her gaze and saw that the coming from the North was someone covered in flames riding on the shoulders of some sort of stone beast and behind him came Black Machines that chewed and devoured the ground and behind them came a vast army of people and behind them there was only fire.

So much fire.

    Brin took up a defensive position in front of the Queen and as he did two War Pandas came forward and stood to each side as well. Messy had seen battles before, had seen bad times but never, never in her worst nightmares had she believed it would come to this. She watched horrified as the army of the West attacked the Northern armies and fell before the Black Machines and the fire that the leader of that army shot out of what looked like a scepter. Messy clutched the box tighter and looked at Beliar; unsure what to say to her daughter, unsure what there was to say as all around them the armies clashed.

But there was hope.

As the invading armies approached more and more villagers appeared from the West and with them came more of the Pandas and other creatures of the Kingdom, things that had remained hidden from view for so long Messy had thought they were all gone from these lands but here they were to fight and to protect their home. When Messy looked at her daughter though she barely recognized her. She looked wild.

"Oh honey, what's wrong? What's happening to you?"

"Mother nothing is wrong. These people want war then I will show them the face of war."

Beli closed her eyes and mouthed a word and in an instant she erupted into black flames that coursed over her body and writhed as if they were a living thing. Beli reached out and squeezed her mother's hand and then turned and ran off towards the Southern front of the battle. Messy looked down at her hand and saw it was red where her daughter had touched her.

The world flashed past Beli but she saw none of it. She acted on instinct alone and dodged explosions and beasts from the other Kingdoms as they tried to attack her. Everything was a roar of white noise but as soon as Beli entered the fray of battle the world of her enemies erupted into an inferno of black flames that was a flood that swallowed everything in its path burning all of the invading forces but leaving the forces of the crown untouched. Ahead of her the Warlocks from the South fired their conjuring stones at her but when they saw Beli the terrible looks of satisfaction they wore faded. None of the dark magic had an effect on Beli or the black fire and as she approached them the Warlocks all fell before her and begged for mercy she would not give and the world of the Southern front became a nightmare of flames around them. She raised her arms to rain fire on everything but then all around her there appeared several beautiful women bathed in white who formed a circle around Beli and the Warlocks. A woman amongst the group stepped forward and she looked so much like her mother that she knew who she was in an instant.

"Grandma?"

Anamare stepped forward and reached into the black flames and took her granddaughter's hands in her own.

"This is not the way, Beliar."

"This is what I am, this is *all* I am. Look what they are doing; what do you want me to do? What can I do but this?" Beli pleaded.

"I want you to lead."

"But how? How can I do that now, here?"

"By showing mercy to those that deserve it and understanding that we are always more than we see. We are better than our worst, and have more in us than we often realize. Don't let these people, or this war change who you are. You choose your path. Use this gift not as a weapon but as a tool."

"But, but all I want is to hurt them. To hurt

them for what they've done." Beli was crying uncontrollably.

"Then look past that, past your hate, to them and why they did what they did. Look past and see if there is something more to them than the hate that you find trying to work its spell on you."

Beli felt a jolt pass from her grandmother's hands to her own and she saw the people before her not as her enemies but as people, people misled into being here, into being a part of this war. People dirty, battered, and scared. Yes, the Warlocks were monsters, ancient things that lived to destroy but they too were pathetic beneath their robes and magic. Anamare let go of her granddaughter and stepped back into the circle of women and then was gone. Beli looked down at her hands and the flames that dripped from them and then at the people kneeling before her. Behind them, around them lay dozens of their people. These were all that remained. Beli closed her eyes and lifted a hand and the Warlocks screamed. She opened her eyes and saw that all of their hands had been burned and they were holding them close to their bodies trying to stop the pain. Beli looked at their conjuring stones and she made a fist and all of them shattered to dust. She turned her attention back to the people of the South.

 "Go. Go home. Take your wounded and dead and go home while you can."

Beli turned and began walking back to her mother and from behind her she heard the sounds of movement and knew they were doing as she had told them. Beli saw several soldiers fighting for the crown start to follow the Southerners and she shook her head at them and pointed to the other battles and the people nodded and headed in those directions instead.

The Southern front was safe.

When Beli returned to her mother Messy saw that she still looked different but that she also looked like her daughter again, like a young Princess facing a desperate time. Messy took her daughter's hand and they looked out at the chaos unfolding around them. The War Pandas were fighting the Blurrgs and already one of the great monsters had fallen, though it had taken many of the Pandas down itself. To the North the Black Machines were spreading out and decimating everything that came before them and those that did not fall to them fell to the screaming man leading the army. The fire that followed engulfing and encircling all but the Western front. The army from the Carnival Kingdom were fighting the army of the East to a stalemate until people of the Kingdom joined them and pushed them back and back and then more animals and beasts came to join. Just as it looked as if the battle to the East was about to turn one of the Black Machines came from behind and joined. Beliar moved to join as well but was held in place by Brin.

"We saw what you did Princess. What you can do. Stay. You must stay and protect your mother. They are coming for your mother." Brin said.

"No, no, they'll take me but they want the Palace. They want the symbol for the Kingdom and the Queens…and the Mistresses of Magic. We are simply what stands in their way. They will burn the citadel and then take or kill me. That is their plan." Messy responded.

From behind the group there was a loud crash and a howl. Beli saw movement out of the corner of her eye and looked and saw that one of the Blurrgs had gotten free of its foes and had made it to the Palace. It was a third as tall as her home which made it nearly forty feet tall and it had used its large, flat head to smash through a side wall at the space where she and her sister's rooms were. Messy screamed and threw her hand up as if to ward the thing off but it was too late because it was already smashing its head into the building again and then again. More of the Palace shattered, cracked, and fell apart as the white stones that had been used to build it were crushed under the impact of the beast. Beli turned and saw that the other Blurrg was keeping the armies busy and the rest were being occupied by the surging Northern army, which had been joined by a small handful of Southern Warlocks who had broken from their brethren to join that front. Another crash and Beli looked at the Palace and saw that there was a fire where the kitchen used to be. Above there was a small window of sunlight that had broken through the darkness but it was quickly blotted out by things Beli had never seen before, things that looked as if they were part tree and which dropped from the sky to pick up villagers or Pandas and took them off into the flames, only to emerge without their prey.

They had to act.

Beli looked at her mother and Messy, tears in her eyes, nodded and Beli ran towards the Palace and erupted into flames as she ran. When she was near enough to smell the thing she clenched her hands into fists and swung her arms forward as if they held rocks and threw bolts of fire at the Blurrg and set it ablaze. The thing howled with pain and Beli saw the fear in it, the confusion and she screamed but as she did she felt the coldness she had felt from her grandmother fill her arms and without thinking she raised them and held them out towards the Palace and the beast and white light slashed out and hit the fire and put it out instantly. The Blurrg let out a pitiful howl and fell onto the side and was surrounded by Pandas. Beli ran forward and pushed her way to the monster, which was still alive but was wounded from the fire and the battle. She fell to her knees and put her hands on the Blurrg's face and it was crying just as she was and it was in so much pain it felt like fire inside her chest. She closed her eyes and let the tears come and felt the cold running down her arms like water, running down onto the Blurrg and all over it and she heard it let out a low moan and stop moving and her eyes snapped open and the thing before here was no longer covered in blood and soot but was clean and healed and was looking at her with eyes that were no longer a beast's but were the eyes of something thinking, feeling, and very afraid. Beli felt sick and swooned and fell to the side but felt a strong claw catch her and she was held aloft as the Blurrg slowly rolled over and rose, making sure not to let the girl fall as it did. The Pandas and humans that had surrounded it backed up but did not act because they too saw it was different. It was no longer a monster. The Blurrg steadied Beli and then rose to its full height and let out a fearsome roar and looked down at Beliar, who felt weak. Beli opened her eyes and the Blurrg was shining as if covered in gold and she locked eyes with it a moment and she knew what it was going to do in an instant but could do nothing to stop it. It dropped its eyes and roared again and leapt over the group surrounding it and ran for the Black Machines.

The Blurrg pounced on the first machine it came upon and tore it apart with its powerful paws, the machine letting out a blood curdling scream as it died. The beast moved to the next and did the same, over and over and over, its paws covered in the thick black goo that powered the monstrosities as one by one they fell before it. Beli tried to stand but couldn't and fell to her knees but was helped up again by the Pandas that had caught her and she followed the sounds and wreckage to the Blurrg, which was still fighting furiously. The animal was working on the last of the Black Machines and had it on its knees but before it could finish destroying it the Blurrg was set upon by the beasts from above which bit and tore at it and by the Northern Army, who beat it and set it on fire. The Blurrg let out a terrible howl of pain and Beli screamed with it. The Blurrg turned and locked eyes with Beliar and she felt its mind, its heart and it was happy, dying but happy to die free, to have chosen to fight whatever the cost. The fire intensified for a moment and when the fire dissipated the creature was gone and all that remained was ash and the machine, which was wounded but limped forward against the crown. The surviving Blurrg let out its own mournful cry at the loss of its brother and suddenly the spell on it was broken and it ran at the last machine but was mortally wounded and collapsed not far from the other. Beli felt a cramp fill her stomach and she quickly looked to her mother and saw that Brin was dead at her feet with a spear in him and the two Pandas were either dead or unconscious and the Queen was being held by the throat by the man who led the North.

The Son looked at Beliar and motioned for her to come near.

"Come. Come here and let's end this now. Yes?"

He spoke quietly but despite the thunderous sound of the machine, the battle, and the fire in the Palace Beliar could hear him clearly.

He was tall and lean and looked skeletal with his eyes sunken into his burned face. Had he not spoken she would not have known he had a mouth at all because when closed it disappeared into his many scars. Upon his head was a halo of sticks covered in cobwebs and around his shoulders was a robe of writhing flames that sent out black light that covered him in a cloud. Beli looked at him and knew what he was - Son. This was Lady Hush's son. Her heir. She looked into him and saw only black.

Darkness.

Nothing.

There was nothing in him but fire, a fire he wanted to spread across the world.

She stood her ground and saw him frown and he lifted her mother up by her throat.

"Fine. Have it your way. You'll die, like her, like all of your people. You can do it now. You can do it later. It doesn't matter to me. I have forever." He lifted the Queen even higher and Beli watched as the blood drained from her mother's face.

"NO!" One of Brin's people ran at the Son from behind but with a glance from the crown's enemy the man was dropped and in flames and all attention was on Beli again.

Beli felt alive with black fire, wanting to burn everything and everyone that dared to hurt her mother and her people. She was alive with rage. She held onto the white light though as tightly as she could and focused on the Son. This was one that she would not spare. This was one that she would not shed a tear over. She mustn't lose herself though, not to the rage, if she did that she was but a mirror image of the creature before her. She began walking towards the Son slowly and smiled as the voice of his mother screamed in her mind, taunting her and screaming at her. The more Hush screamed the wider Beli's smile became and the more fiercely the fire in her burned. The battle raged on around Beliar and out of the corner of her eye she saw the remaining people of the Carnival Kingdom surround and destroy the last of the Black Machines and then turn their attention on the army that had followed behind. Something slipped from the Queen's hands and crashed onto the marble. It was the box she had made. Beli started to rush forward to grab the box but stopped herself, though too late. The Son looked down at his feet, curious. He dropped Messy in an unconscious heap on the ground and bent down to look at what had fallen. He had three soldiers from the North that flanked him but they stood still, like zombies, or as if they were under a spell. The Son laughed as he looked at what lay before him.

"A box? A *box*? That is what you bring to a war, my Queen? Oh dear. A shame more of your Meep Sheep didn't survive until now or perhaps you could sic them on me as well. They could cuddle me to death. Enough toys. Enough games. Enough."

The Son lifted his bare foot up and brought it down heavily on the box and shattered it and out of it fell a small green ball. Messy moaned and reached out to the ball but the Son laughed at her and lifted his foot to shatter that as well.

Beli heard a voice in their head, their mother's voice – *The Queen's Tears. You must protect the Queen's Tears!*

Beli raised her arms to shoot the black fire at him but before she could a blast of white light hit the Son and he screamed in pain. Beli's mouth dropped open and she saw Aribel coming up the steps towards the Son from his blind side and behind her were Pandas and humans and another army she didn't recognize. The army of the North immediately engaged the new army and the battle began anew. The fire that had been marching across the land had arrived and had begun to engulf the Northern hills and was moving to consume everything to the East and West. The Son stood back up and sent a bolt of fire at Ari but Beli destroyed it before it could touch her, the black flame happy to be released. Ari ran to Beli and they grabbed one another's hands.

The Son's face was split with an awful grin.

"It's no matter. Let the witches come. You can all die together, like your, ah, yes, your father. You can all burn...but please, feel free to try something against me and I will be more than happy to make sure your mother goes first."

The Son held out his arms and the windows of the Palace exploded outwards and the tallest spire shattered as a fireball erupted from it. The girls turned and their hearts broke in unison as their home became fully engulfed in flame. Around them the troops of the North marched up the steps and surrounded them, and with them the last four of the Southern Warlocks, who turned anyone that opposed them to stone. Beli heard a cry from the field below and saw a group of Pandas rushing to break through the enemies from behind.

Ari leaned in to her sister.

"The Thicket. If we can get to the Thicket and get our back to it they cannot surround us. We may yet have a chance there."

As she said that though they heard the laughter of the Son and turned to see him pointing beyond them, to the West and so they turned to look and used everything they had to keep from screaming.

Filling the Western front like a great cancer was a tree of enormous size that towered into the sky and was as wide as the Palace and covered in flowers of green flame. Beli had never seen anything like it and was horrified to see it. It used its branches to pull itself forward as its roots would snake out and find purchase before moving so that it dragged itself closer and closer and closer by the moment. There were things like boils that covered the tree and as the tree moved the boils would pop and thick, black sap would run down the trunk to create small rivers and from the rivers came hideous things that looked half-formed, things that were part tree and part animal and that crawled, flew, and walked in the trail of their parent towards the fight. Worst of all was that there were that there were several Pandas with the tree.

Pandas who wore dark red as war paint and who were serving a monster.

"Ladies and gentleman, I present the face of your destruction, meet the Great Loneliness…" Said the Son with a smile.

There was a moment of silence as all fighting stopped and everyone watched the tree approach. In a moment the tree began to speak as it moved forward, its speech coming in bursts as it wheezed heavily.

"I…have come…a…great distance…to see you all…die. I…was here before any of you, was here at the beginning. I have waited…waited…waited for this day when I could…could…end this tyranny. I…I…Darkness. We shall send you all…into the fire…and after the fire there shall be darkness. Oh…for those…those that worry…the Panda Tree…the Bumble Tree…the Thicket…and all that lived in that place…are gone…as dead as the Thicket itself. Now…let come the fire…Let come the Darkness."

The Great Loneliness let out a long breath that came as a hiss and its minions sprang forward, hundreds, thousands of things that turned their attentions to the battle that had become a stalemate but which quickly turned again towards the Son and the Great Loneliness. Ari saw that it was clear that the forces that fought for the Kingdom were weary and battered but raised their weapons and some ran to meet the new foes while the rest continued the fight against the last remnants of the East and the North. It was hard not to cough from the thick smoke that was rolling forward from the fires that were spreading and many from both sides were succumbing to it. Ari looked from the battlefield towards the great tree and saw that the Loneliness had stopped and its roots were digging their way into the earth as it rooted itself and as it did all the ground around it turned black with rot. Its branches lashed out and anyone or anything that got close was snatched up and crushed or thrown into the fire, be they those fighting for the crown or those children of the tree it cared not. It just wanted to destroy. As Ari watched the rot began to spread as quickly as the fire and the Palace and battlefield were becoming surrounded. What was worse and more immediate was that the Whisper Wagon her father lay in was in danger of being trampled in the battle.

Beli wanted to act but something told her to wait, to wait and to have faith. It came like a cool breeze on her ear so she held back and squeezed her sister's hand and tried to breathe slowly and wait.

Wait, said the voice in her ear and Ari

nodded as if she had heard it also, though neither thought that they had much time left to wait.

When it all happened it was a blur.

The Son had turned and to watch as the war began to turn towards the North and the Great Loneliness and as the Son was distracted the Queen, who everyone had forgotten, was up in an instant and on him, pulling a small glass ball from a bag slung around her shoulder and smashing it onto his chest. As she did this The Pandas standing beside the girls threw their spears and took care of the guards standing with the Son. The Son let out a scream of anguish and pushed the Queen away forcibly and as she fell backwards he shot a bolt of fire at her that pierced her chest. She opened her mouth and nothing came out and by the time she hit the ground she was silent. The girls ran to their mother and as they ran Beli shot black fire into the Son and Ari shot white fire. He fell hard to his knees and then fell forward, his own flames pouring out of his mouth and into a pool before him. From the battlefield there came yelling near the Great Loneliness and the girls looked up to see that there was another army rushing to enter the fray now. It looked like the entire Panda Kingdom was coming on the backs of enormous Giraffes that galloped quickly towards the children of the Loneliness and with the Pandas came thousands of humans. From behind the girls limped Arnk and he moved to their mother and lifted her head. He shook his head from side to side and looked at the girls, whose faces were a mess of tears and soot. Arnk ran a hand over the Queen's face and wiped the dirt from her brow. Behind them the Son was screaming and around them all was smoke and fire. Arnk shook his head again and lifted the Queen's head higher and clenched his teeth and whispered into Messy's ear and then pulled away again. He looked to the sky and threw a hand in the air and let out a high whistle and from out of the darkness there came a Meep Sheep and then he let out another whistle and a Kreep Sheep came and both animals landed to either side of Arnk and stood next to him and the fallen Queen. Ari went to him and he waved her off.

"I need time. Space and time. Look after…" But before he could finish everyone realized that the Son was gone, stumbling away, towards the writhing and raging black tree.

The Great Loneliness roared with laughter that quickly stopped. It had poisoned the Thicket and its children and now it would poison the world and it had expected resistance. It had hoped for resistance. It hadn't expected this though. The black tree roared with rage and swept Giraffes and Pandas alike aside and those that made it past were swallowed by the black sludge but still the opposition surged forward. Men ran forward carrying severed tree trunks that they lay down as makeshift bridges across the black sludge and people and animals alike rushed across to enter the battle. Atop the lead Giraffe rode the Great Loof, who swung a shock-mace and he took down all flying beasts that dared come near. At his side was his daughter Skraw. They came to the exiled Pandas that had helped to fell the Panda Tree and that had betrayed the Panda Kingdom and Skraw leapt from her steed and took out Praw with one stroke of her sword. Loof climbed down slowly and faced Zum himself.

"Old man, it is long past time that your kind gave up this land and returned to the void where you belong."

"Is that so, oh Zum? Is that what we should

do?"

"How do you know my name, old man?" Zum asked as he circled around the Panda King.

"I know you because my mother helped birth you and my father was friends with yours and because there was a time when I looked after you as if you were of my own cub. Had I known now what you would become I never would have saved you from the black pool you had fallen into as a cub." Loof replied.

"That, that, that was you that saved me? That was..." Zum lowered his weapon.

"Yes, it was." Loof struck Zum once in the chest with the shock-mace but as he attacked a great black thing that looked like a beetle lifted and swallowed the Great Loof and he was gone before Zum had hit the ground dead.

Skraw's eyes grew wide and she became a whirlwind of rage on seeing her father's death and nothing that stood before her survived.

The Son stumbled through the crowds battling towards the Great Loneliness and fell on his knees before it, the cold grasp of death winding its way around him. The Son had never known fear before but the coldness from the fire the girls had burned him with was not leaving and he couldn't stop shaking and with that there was a second beating in his chest, as if from a second heart. The witch, the witch had done something to him and everywhere he looked there was white fire that came from the bodies of the fallen. As he watched, body twitching the dead began to rise, one by one and one by one they all turned their gazes on him. The Son screamed out.

"Mother! Mother protect me. MOTHER!

PLEASE!"

There was silence. His mother had stopped speaking to him during the battle and there came only silence now. He was alone.

He lifted his arms to the great black tree and begged for aid.

"Please. Please. Please...don't let it end like this...in cold...let it end in fire...Please, you promised me, you promised..."

From behind him came a voice that sounded like cracking timber.

"No. It does not end with cold, or with fire. For you...it ends with dirt."

The Son turned in time to see a tree that for a moment looked like a woman come up from behind him and wrap its branches around and around and around him and once it had him it rooted itself into the ground then began to sink down into the mud. The Son tried to scream but as soon as he opened his mouth it was filled with dirt and in a matter of moments he was gone and then the tree was gone and all that remained of both was a scorched place where they had been and the last thought he had was of his father and how they would never be together. Then the Son and his fire were gone.

The fire and the black rot were coming closer and closer and it was clear something had to stop it or it would be too late for those that were still fighting. Beli and Ari looked around but saw nothing that could help, nothing that could solve their problems. Nothing...then they both saw it at once, the small green stone lying forgotten on the ground. The girls ran for the stone and Ari grabbed it and held it up, hoping, praying she would feel something alive, would feel *something* that would help them but there was nothing. Nothing. She closed her eyes and tears burned behind her lids. Beli came up to her and wrapped her arms around her sister and squeezed her.

"Ari, maybe this isn't for us to do. Maybe this was about mom. Or dad. Or I don't know."

"But Beli, Beli I thought, I thought it was our time…"

"Whoever said it wasn't your time?" Came a voice both girls knew.

They looked past the stone and saw their grandmother and the other women bathed in white.

"Why are you here? Why are all of you here?" Asked Beliar.

"When the Great Loneliness awoke the Mother Wood woke us from our slumber, calling us back to protect our people. You girls are the future of this Kingdom and that future begins now and it only begins if you both work together. This land and its people have lost so much, it's time to stop the pain and to heal. It's time for everyone to heal...and it starts with you girls."

"But how?" Asked Ari.

"By being the spark of life for the seed you hold."

Queen Anamare and the other Mistresses of Magic grew bright then brighter still and then were gone and the girls suddenly knew what they must do. Beliar and Aribel looked out over the ruins of the only place they had known as home. They place they had laughed, cried, and for Beli, had fallen in love. But they were only teenagers still and to see the faces of the people that fought for this Kingdom, for their homes and families and the lives they had worked and bled for made them understand something their mother

had learned in the first year of being Queen –
the people were what mattered and nothing
more. It was the people that made a
Kingdom, not the Kingdom that made the
people. Messy had gone to the neighboring
Kingdoms time and again during her first
years in power to renew the vows of peace
and to forge friendships where there had not
been any for decades. Her own mother had
been too busy raising a daughter and
changing the way that the Kingdom of Man
ran for diplomacy so many of the ties between
nations had cracked. Anamare had focused
her efforts on moving the Kingdom of Man
away from war preparations. She knew that
she must safeguard against war but live at
peace or the nations around them would
never do the same. In both cases it was about
the people. It was about people. All of it. And
now the girls both saw how this fight was not
about them or their mother, even if the Son
and the Great Loneliness wanted it to be

about them, no, it was about these people, all of these people willing to die for their homes and loved ones. The girls looked down at their mother, whose hair was a dozen shades of gray, and who was so still as the Meep and Kreep Sheep sniffed her and nudged her softly with their heads. Arnk was whispering into their mother's ear and as they watched she nodded and opened her eyes a little and smiled at Aribel and Beliar and they returned it. A wind picked up and the smoke and the fire rose higher and licked at the low ceiling.

"Is dad…" Asked Beli, whispering so no one else would hear.

"No, but I don't know if he'll last the night if we don't find some way to heal him."

"What happened?"

"The Daughter." Ari replied.

"That…"

"It isn't like you think. The Daughter isn't what you think. None of this is what any of us thought it was."

Beli turned to face her sister, confused.

"This is a lie, all of it. A lie born with the Great Loneliness and passed to Hush and from her passed to her children and to the rest of the Kingdoms. A lie that there is darkness, a vast, great darkness that will hide us from our pain. But there isn't. The only darkness is within ourselves, and that which we force upon others. Beli *we* create the darkness. We do. And we can undo it."

Ari smiled at her sister and took her hand once more as she made a fist around the green stone with her other hand. Beliar put her own hand around the stone and both felt the stone start to vibrate in their hands. With both girls holding it the stone began vibrating and it became so fierce that the girls thought it would tear itself from their hands but it remained and started to grow warm. The girls closed their eyes and their minds were one and they saw themselves pouring their energy into the stone, their black fire and white fire, pouring it into it until the stone could take no more, until they could take no more and when they opened their eyes the thing in their hands was pulsing with green light, beating as if it were a heart.

"The Queen's Tears." Both girls said, speaking in unison before each kissed the stone.

"But how…" Asked Ari.

"I will do it." Replied Beli.

They knew what they must do and Beliar knew how she needed to do it. She could finally try to make amends for what she had done years earlier. She could finally close that book forever. Ari nodded to her sister and they let go of one another and then Ari let get of the stone. Beli made a fist around the stone and then knelt and began gathering the mud and ash that littered the marble pavers into a pile and then she awkwardly began to form the mess into a snake that measured nearly four feet long. When it was done she put the stone in one end and then laid her hands on either side of it and she sent a jolt of the black fire into it. She stood up slowly and watched it and for a moment it was still but then it began to twitch, to shake, and then rose up and wavered faceless before Beli. Beliar bent forward and whispered into the side of the thing where its ear might have been and then she kissed it and before it fell back down to the marble and slithered away from the girls and down the steps towards the great black tree.

Beliar's snake slithered between

combatants and over and through the obstacles and towards the tree. It was almost to the Great Loneliness when a branch slashed through the air and impaled the snake and then another came and ripped it in half. The snake was still a moment but then melted into several pools of black fire that surged over the branches and then re-united and became a snake once more and returned to its mission. The black tree raged and roared and sent more branches at it but each one was avoided and proved to be nothing more than nuisances. Finally the snake made it to the black pool and easily glided through it and then it slithered up and up and up the trunk and the Great Loneliness let out a moan and began driving branches into itself as it tried to stop the snake. One, two, three, more and more branches drove into the trunk and thick green sap drained out of it and the black tree

slumped forward and wheezed. The Great
Loneliness tried to uproot itself, to get away
but it was dug in too deeply. The children of
the Great Loneliness stopped battling the
enemies of their father and turned to watch
what was happening as the tree fought itself.
Seeing their father was in trouble the
creatures all rushed back to the tree but it
was too late. The snake found a small
knothole near the top of the tree and slid
quickly inside before one last branch could
stop it. The branch impaled the back end of
the snake but the snake shed its tale and
slithered in and was gone. There was a
moment of silence then as the tree lashed at
itself and slammed its thick branches against
its body but then it stopped moving
altogether and the Great Loneliness let out a
horrible hissing sound and green fluid began
to pour from the knothole and every little hole
within the trunk, fluid that quickly became a
river then a flood that joined with the black

river and then overpowered it. The children of the Great Loneliness ran into the green fluid with fear only for their parent but they were immediately stuck within it as if it was quicksand and in moments they all disappeared from the world as the fluid devoured them. The green fluid became a flood that poured from the tree. The servants of the Kingdom tried to run from the fluid but they too were caught in it but for them the fluid went around them and rushed forward and out and the allies to the crown easily extracted themselves and turned their attention to follow the rush of liquid. The raging fire had decimated the Kingdom but was nothing to the flood of the fluid and was consumed by it and became nothing but great clouds of smoke that rose into the sky.

The Great Loneliness let out a terrible last howl of pain and then the fire flowers that had covered its skin all went out and one last hiss escaped the tree and then it was silent.

With the Son and the Great Loneliness gone the enemies from the North stopped fighting, dropped their weapons and fell to their knees begging for mercy. Many of them broke into tears to see the battlefield and to know what they had done. The fluid went out and out and out, across the valley, across the plains, and out into the distance. There was a quiet that hung heavy in the air as all eyes watched the black tree turn white and its branches stretched outward from the trunk and rose and stretched into the sky, breaking through the smoke and rising higher and higher and higher. There came a great crash of thunder that rolled across the Kingdom, and then another and then a slash of lightning that lit up the world and then came the rain, the softest, sweetest rain that ever fell. Slowly the smoke was torn apart by the rain and the green fluid was washed away and as the people of all the Kingdoms slowly left the battlefield and gathered at the remains of the Palace and the base of the white tree, unsure what they were seeing but knowing it was important. Knowing it was something that would change everything.

The branches of the white tree spread out wide over the people below and as the rain fell small green buds began to cover every inch of the long arms of the tree. As the people and animals all watched the tree became covered with leaves and buds. From those buds burst multi-colored flowers that opened as the rain ended and all across the Kingdom new grass and trees were growing to cover the scarred landscape with new life.

Ari and Beli saw none of this, nor did they hear the sounds of the people as their murmuring talk became the roar of cheers and laughter as far above the cloud cover cracked open and split apart. The sisters were more concerned about their parents. Beliar ran to the Whisper Wagon where her father was and Aribel ran to her mother to check on her. The Meep Sheep and Kreep Sheep were chasing each other around and around Messy and Arnk and it was clear that Ari's mother was doing better. The Queen was awake and blinking and she smiled weakly at her daughter when she saw her.

"Where is your father?"

Ari turned and looked towards the Wagon and Messy pushed Arnk and a Panda away and slowly rose and started walked towards her husband. The Kreep Sheep and Meep Sheep, the last two of their species after having been the very first followed along weaving in and out of one another's paths playfully. Messy stumbled but caught the marble rail and walked on but when she stumbled again it was Ari that caught her and the two of them made their way down the stairs. Ari noticed Skraw on her knees and crying with her father's sword in one hand and her brother's spear in the other. And this was the cost of the war. This was the glory. Ari and Messy both knelt and hugged Skraw and she wrapped her own large arms around the women but then nodded towards the Whisper Wagon and the King.

Beli was crying and when Ari saw this she felt a scream rush up her throat but before it could break the surface her mother grabbed her arm and Ari saw the reason that her sister was crying.

The King lived.

The King lived.

Their father was alive.

Messy and Aribel ran the last few feet to Vix and Beliar and the four of them grabbed one another and none could stop the tears as they ran but their reunion was interrupted by an old friend with one last message.

"Your Majesties, much has been lost in this war, much has been sacrificed, and many of the things and people that made this Kingdom beautiful have been lost forever. But even forever may have an end. Look to the White Tree and perhaps you shall find some manner of solace and a small spark of light in these dark times. I take my leave of you to tend to the wounded."

Arnk bowed to the royal family and stepped aside and the people of the four Kingdoms were standing under the White Tree as from it fell multicolored seeds that split open as they hit the ground and from them came the creatures of the Thicket Pandas, Giraffes, Bumble Kitties, Bloo Moos and more. With each new seed that fell and opened into an animal there rose a cheer from the crowd. It was a start.

It was a start.

And so the war was over.

PART FOUR

As the sky cleared and the last remnants of a sun that had not been seen in weeks appeared it was then that a weakened Messy spoke to the crowd of people that only continued to grow on the still healing lawn of the citadel. Behind her the Palace still smoked from the fire and damaged that had scarred it but the sky was full of Wimblers, Bumble Kitties, and other creatures, the Kreep Sheep and Meep Sheep choosing instead to lie at their mistresses' feet.

"Whatever becomes of this day in the annals of our joined histories the losses that were suffered will echo for all time. We have lost so much. We have lost so many. Let us take heart though for if the White Tree is a sign then perhaps the darkness has passed. Let us then all hold a candle and let the light of it remind us that there is always hope, even on the blackest of days and let our candles be a reminder of the many lives that were lost during this last war. Once, when the world was still young we were all creatures from the same tree and members of the same tribe. Now, with the borders broken, with all of the Kingdoms mortally wounded, with all of us broken in heart and spirit perhaps this war, this terrible war will remind us of those early days when once we were all family and all of one tribe and let us never forget that it is this tree that has given us a second chance at light and life."

Messy felt light headed but kept her composure as she spoke and when she was done she stepped away from the railing and was helped to a chair nearby. The crowds had been growing and growing throughout the evening, people from all the Kingdoms making their way to the citadel of the Kingdom of Man to make their apologies and to look for family and friends who may have survived the war. No one quite understood what had happened, why they had wanted this war, why they had fought it, and why so many had died for a thing that none could understand. All any of them could recall was the voice of a woman telling them to fight, fight, *fight*. After so much loss and so much pain, there was no more hate or anger left in anyone and the people and animals began to help one another and to bandage each other's wounds and in the end it was stories and laughter that filled the night as the tales of the told times were told late into the night.

Not everything was laughter though as the royal families and leaders that of the Kingdoms that still remained gathered together to say goodbye to friends and loved ones and gave tribute to the many lost in the war. It was during these ceremonies that there was one last surprise as bleeding and weary and seriously wounded, Ashley Pickles finally made his way to see the Queen on the back of a Giraffe.

Messy stood as soon as she saw Ash and rushed to him, ignoring the pain in her body, and threw her arms around her old friend when he neared.

"How, how did you make it? How did you survive, Ashley?"

Ash tried to smile but couldn't. His face was bruised and there was a long cut that ran the length of the right side and he was clearly not the same man she had known for these long years.

"I sometimes wonder if I did make it. It all seems like a blur. A nightmare. I was about to be killed by Zum's War Panda, who was content to toy with me a bit before it killed me when a miracle happened. The Thicket had been poisoned and was dying as well as everything in it and all that remained was the black tree. I believed all hope was lost but just as it seemed I would die the Giraffe Kingdom entered the war and charged the Thicket. It is often forgotten what fierce warriors the Giraffes are but they reminded the Great Loneliness and their assault forced the black tree and its children to abandon the Thicket and to assault the Palace leaving some half formed creatures to fight with the Giraffes. With the Giraffes so isolated for all these years none remembered that this was a proud race of warriors that would not back down from a fight which was why they and the Pandas had always kept their distance from one another. Once the remnants of the black tree's children were destroyed the Giraffes came to my aid and I told them what was happening. The Giraffe and Panda wars were terrible but they had managed to stay at peace for several hundred years and while they avoided one another the Giraffes would not stand to see their homeland invaded. I took the Giraffes to see the Great Loof and together the two tribes joined and followed the black tree's path until it led here. And here I am. I have been here since the last battle but was not well enough to come here until now. I needed to see you before I left."

"Left?" Messy asked.

"Left. I am leaving in the morning with the last of the people of the Carnival Kingdom. I am going to visit King Glen and perhaps will retire there, or somewhere else. I find that this land is full of too many ghosts."

"But Ash what about the kitties? You had…"

At this he did smile.

"Don't worry. We are taking some with us, as well as a seed I found for what I believe is a Bumble Tree. I think that there is a Kingdom across the sea that could use more songs and perhaps the kitties and I, and Glen of course, can see that that happens."

"But what about the land beyond the Thicket? Who will?"

Ash smiled.

"The Giraffe Kingdom and the Panda Kingdom have pledged to set a watch all along what remains of the Thicket and there was talk that the Dire Rhinos may come from the East to join the watch. We are not ready for what lies beyond the Thicket and until we are that place must be guarded above all else. The Thicket gave its life to protect that Kingdom beyond we must be willing to do the same. If what I heard by the fire tonight is true though it is said that this strange rain has made it so that even the Thicket is growing back, which would be a sight to see, though one I will leave for other eyes to witness."

Messy leaned forward and squeezed Ash again and kissed both cheeks.

"I am sorry to see you go, Ashley. Very sorry. I hope though that for this night, this last night, you'll lend us your company and perhaps sing a song."

"My Queen I would be honored. Now where are the girls, where is your husband?"

"The girls are there, at the railing, watching the butterbugs and the people. Vix is sleeping. He was badly injured in the battle. He cannot move well but the doctors say that in a few weeks he will be on his feet again but he will never fully heal. He will adjust, he just needs time. I suppose we all do."

"I suppose we do. Now, if I am going to sing I better go get something to drink first, so for now I bid you farewell but not goodbye. I shall see you in a bit."

Messy nodded and watched Ash limp away.

"Was that Mr. Pickles, mom? It looked like him but he looked…different." Beliar asked.

"Yes, honey, that was Ash. I am afraid things took a toll on him as well. He is leaving tomorrow and wanted to see us before he left. But he will be with us tonight, which makes me very happy."

"Us too." The girls responded.

Messy wavered and the girls wrapped their arms around her and the three of them watched the sky and the firebugs and the flamebees that zig-zagged through the night. The girls helped Messy back to her chair and then they sat on the ground before her and suddenly these young women who would one day very soon be Queens of this land if they chose to be were her little girls again and she smiled.

"What is it mom?" Asked Beli.

"Just smiling at how beautiful you both are."

The girls grinned shyly.

"Mom, what about the Mistresses? What about you? Will you still go to the Mother Wood? Is it still there?" Ari asked her mother.

Messy shook her head.

"I don't know. I know that the Mistresses are still here and I can feel them in the White Tree. I know that I heard the voice of my mother when I was dying, and that it was she that called me back and Arnk that kept me here. I know that even in the darkness there was light, and at its heart was the White Tree. As for what becomes of me, I don't know. I can feel that my days as Queen are at an end but beyond that I am not sure yet. I suppose time will tell. I do know that you both have some very serious decisions to make."

"I don't want you to leave." Said Beli from behind her hair.

"I know, my dear. I know. But all things must change eventually. I am not leaving yet though. You girls still need to make some very hard decisions on what you will do when I am gone and the throne sits empty."

Messy gave the girls a serious look and the girls held her gaze and as they did they both saw their paths, and what decision they had to make and as they realized it they dropped their eyes. It was Aribel that broke the silence between them.

"Are, are the Meep Sheeps all gone? All of them?" Asked Ari, her voice choked with tears.

Messy frowned and felt something twist in her chest.

"Yes. And the Kreep Sheeps. All but the Kreep and Meep that are here now. The first of their kinds. The rest were lost to this war. War is a hungry thing and it devours everything unless it is stopped. But yes, they are gone...for now. That doesn't mean that they cannot return - but that is something my daughters will have to see to...when the time is right."

"Mom, may *I* ask you something?" It was Beli's turn to ask now.

"What, my dear?"

"How come you don't talk about when you were a little girl, or when you became Queen? How come you never talk about yourself?"

Messy's face went red to match her hair, which had regained its color and was now the color of the fire that had scorched the land just hours earlier. She had always kept the girls at bay, hoping to protect them, to protect even Vix from the darkness she had seen in the Kingdom, in the other lands, and in herself but in trying to protect them she had pushed them all away.

"Oh girls. I, I suppose I thought I was protecting you. I'm sorry."

"It's ok…" Ari said, though she didn't look at her mother when she said it.

"Girls, let me tell you a story as your is being cared for. A bedtime story because once I tell it you may listen to Ashley sing one song, *one song*, and then it's to bed for both of you. I am still Queen, and still your mother and what I say goes. Got it?" She said this sternly but it was clear that there was a smile beneath her dour look.

"Got it." Said Beli.

"Got it." Said Ari.

"Ok. Now then – Once Upon A Time..."

And so the story began as the Kingdom started the long process of healing wounds that would take decades to mend. The Queen told her daughters the first of what would become many stories of her youth and as she told it one by one people around them sat to listen until hundreds were there listening to this story of the Mistress of Magic but for Messy it was only her daughters that were there and that she spoke to. The King slept peacefully under the stars and dreamt of a beautiful young woman at a Carnival who had stolen his heart. Skraw went to the base of the White Tree and buried the sword and spear and reluctantly went to sit among her people, who all leaned forward to nug her gently on the head one by one before they all shared stories of Loof and Gloof and the other fallen warriors, the Giraffes gathering behind them with their heads bowed as they listened.

Far away over the hills and down a deep shaft the Daughter and the creatures of darkness began to make a world within the middle place between the darkness and the light and started to find a peace within them.

In the nothingness the Lady Hush was silent and still and alone in the darkness, the rage gone and replaced with sorrow for her lost son and sadness for her daughter who would no longer speak to her. She had lost everything, her home, her mate, her children, and now her armies, who had done anything she had asked. Now no one heard her and her dark magic was gone, burned up in a doomed war. She was alone in her own distant edge of the void and forever would be. Silent. Powerless. Alone.

And far, far above the Kingdom of Man flew a lone Meep Sheep and a lone Kreep Sheep who chased each other through the sky and brought balance to a world that had seen the edge and had found its way back.

These were the last sheep.

But not for long.

And yes there was darkness but at the end of every dark night must come the dawn and the sun with it and with that dawn a new story and a new chance to hope and to dream and to create magic.

And magic, oh, magic is never gone; it is just hiding, waiting for us to find it.

But for now, for now this is the end.

Feb. 1 – 2013 ------ March 8 - 2013

HAPPILY EVER AFTER

Thank you to my wife, my family, my many friends and to all of you.

When I started writing I would never have dreamed I would have published ten books (there's a sneaky one in there that isn't for sale but was indeed published). This has all been a dream and the dream exists because of the support of a LOT of people.

Special thanks go out to Miss Messy Stench, Mr. Ashley Peacock, and Miss Amanda Emery (now Ringler). These three inspired characters in these books (and me as I wrote them) and while the books can never hope to capture the magic in these people I hope they serve as a testament to the influence these three have had on my life.

The world of the Meep Sheep, and the many people and creatures that live there goes on, and on, and on. This is but the end to these stories but there are a million stories unwritten. All you need is to close your eyes and you will hear their song.

Thanks.

- Chris Arrrr – March, 2014

Also By **CHRIS RINGLER**

<u>Back from Nothing</u>

<u>This Beautiful Darkness</u>

<u>The Meep Sheep</u>

<u>Red Dreams</u>

<u>The Kreep Sheep</u>

<u>Noches De Corazones Negros</u>

<u>A Shadow Over Ever</u>

<u>Cemetery Earth</u>

and...

<u>The Last Sheep</u> –

aka *The Last War*

These books are but doors - you are the key.
You are always the key.

Safe travels my friends. Safe travels.

Made in the USA
Columbia, SC
11 March 2018